MW01134122

IN THE
SHADOWS
OF THE
Ghost People

BARBARA TYNER HALL

Copyright © 2022 Barbara Tyner Hall
All rights reserved
First Edition

PAGE PUBLISHING
Conneaut Lake, PA

First originally published by Page Publishing 2022

This book is a work of fiction. Names, characters, places, and incidents are the product of the author's imagination. Any resemblance to actual events, locations, or persons living or dead is coincidental.

ISBN 978-1-6624-7773-7 (pbk)
ISBN 978-1-6624-7774-4 (digital)

Printed in the United States of America

Barbara Tyner Hall and her masterpiece *The Ghost People of the Everglades* will bring the readers into a dimension where the reality of conflicted morality exists.

The author easily narrated the story, transpiring a reading vibe that feels like friends are sharing life experiences.

Exciting, riveting, and a way of life for some. I can't wait for the next one.

Novels by Barbara Tyner Hall

Death Valley of Texas
The Ghost People of the Everglades
The Most Outrageous
Alligator Poachers

CONTENTS

A CAPTAIN'S PRAYER

By Joseph Daughtry

A Captain's Prayer

Yea though I wallow in the middle of the trough, my vessel she comforts me for she is sound.
While the wind howls all through the night, a constitution builds within me, and gives me strength to persevere over the duty that I am bound.
My mates, they cry for joy as the sun breaks through the night. We are blessed by God's great bounty, the gale's end is now in sight.
While we toil through the day to provide for our loved one's, I shall not forget my sacred vow, the covenant that God has placed upon me, The Captain's hat upon my brow.
The lives he's placed into my hands, the ones who look to me, to make them safe, a successful voyage, their well being rests with me.... Amen.

SPECIAL THANKS

Special thanks to Kent Daniels for supplying some of the stories featured in this book.

PREFACE

Marathon, Florida, is a small island located midway down a chain of islands called the Florida Keys. Let me take you on a journey deep into the dark secret hidden world of the drug smuggling trade that dominated the islands from the Florida Keys to the Ten Thousand Islands off of Everglades National Park. This happened in the early 1970s. The story tells the dangerous glitz and glamorous lifestyles the commercial fishermen had to endure during a decade of the drug smuggling heyday. Running drugs from the fabulous Florida Keys to Everglades City was the most successful and notorious route. Individual captains who had the best reputations were taken advantage of when they attracted some of the largest cartels housed inside Miami's dangerous dark world.

Because the islands were so coveted for their beauty and the access to the open international waterways, it made this a smuggler's paradise. Still, the hidden secret became the needed way to earn a living and complete the lifestyle the local people had grown so accustomed to. The only industry known to the local people who lived here was commercial fishing, making the most knowledgeable captains a prize possession for top-paying positions working with the cartel. These captains also had crews of extremely knowledgeable men who lived and knew the dangerous waters offshore to the Ten Thousand Islands off of Everglades City.

Defiance and adversity do have a certain appeal. The Everglades attitude is very close to "damn right," "I did it," and "I am not a bit sorry." The townspeople of Everglades City are honorable people but live their lives as lawless daredevils that use the high seas as their playground. No job was ever too big for them. The more danger, the more adrenaline, and the more they liked it. You could feel the natives' hostility if you were an outsider, but you did not feel the dread that slips up on you if they catch you alone at night in the streets of their town. A stranger in Everglades City did not have to look far to find defiance. You can almost breathe it in.

Now in Marathon Key, the crew of one of the largest boats was steadily working on readying a fishing vessel named the Star Gazer for a long and lengthy trip that was taking place later that night.

Captain Tom went out to the back where the crew was loading supplies and giving her the once-over to make sure she is in tip-top shape, and everything was in working order. As Tom stepped out on the dock, he could see the sun had set, and the evening star was hanging over the horizon. A sport-fishing vessel's pale outline moved toward Lower Matecumbe Key, triggering the prayers that started up in Tom's head before every trip. Tom prayed for a safe return and that each crew member returns safely to their families. Then he added to the prayer a blessing for each and every one on the boat for a bountiful and healthy payday that each family needs. In closing, Tom always asked God to forgive him for his sins because he knew what he was doing was wrong, and someday it would catch up to him.

Tom then twisted off a bottle cap and threw it in a bucket and downed a bottle of beer to steady his nerves as the approaching time was nearing for them to leave. Tom decided to eat a good hot meal and spend the last of his time with his family before leaving that evening. You never know what these jobs entail. None of us may come back, so any chance to spend time with the family is well respected and needed.

CHAPTER 1

The Star Gazer

The screen door squeaked as Captain Tom moved through it to the rear deck where the Star Gazer was tied up. The planks were rough and small, only large enough to accommodate two people passing each other, trying not to fall in the water and get on the boat. The salt air was thick and sticky. The humidity was high even in this early morning. It's 1:00 a.m., and the docs were still and quiet, not a sound except for the thunder that followed with lightning flashes that lit up the sky with colors ranging from deep purple to black—the noise and the light show would signal an approaching storm. The storm was still off in the distance, sucking moisture from the sea to be sent back down to earth in hard wind-driven rain. Captain Tom was a walking barometer, and he could feel the impending weather change deep in his bones and was rarely wrong about the approaching storm. The moon was full, and it gave off just enough light to see an occasional ripple in the water from fish feeding in the canal leading to the Gulf of Mexico. "Let's get these supplies loaded. We need to be out of here in about twenty minutes," Captain Tom ordered.

In the cover of the dark night sky, the Star Gazer, a massive seventy-eight-foot commercial fishing boat, was dressed in the standard reel and longline fishing gear mounted on the back of the boat. She was now making her way through four-foot seas, heading for the open waters of the Gulf of Mexico toward the Marquesas. There was a light north cool breeze blowing, and on the horizon, you could see the weather was getting worse. Looking up into the dark and cover of the night, you could see a ring shinning bright around the moon. Fishermen are very superstitious in many ways, and they claim a circle around the moon means there is a storm coming. This confirms what Tom already knew from the aches and pains in his knees, back, and body that he was feeling all day.

"I'm trying to beat the weather here, guys, and make it to our destination before getting too bad out here." Bad weather was nothing to these larger commercial fishing vessels. Captain Tom Charles, a native of the area, knew the water like the back of his hand, given that he has lived here or around the water his whole life. All he knew how to do was work on the water. He started with small boats and worked his way up to owning one of the biggest commercial kingfish and mackerel boats housed at the docks in Marathon, Florida.

This area was teeming with commercial fishing boats that fished for whatever was in season at the time. The old rusty seamen were rough but knowledgeable of what should be happening and what time of the year it should be happening in the local waters. These men were hardworking in a backbreaking, dangerous job. Whatever Mother Nature brought to the workplace for the day is what they had to contend with and suck up because there was no complaining in this field. The crew on the boats depended on the captain as much as they depend on each other to stay safe and return home to their families at night. This was a daily ritual with every boat housed at the seafood companies that the men worked for. Some seasons were short, and some were long, but all had a decent payday attached to them.

CHAPTER 2

Captain Tom Charles

"Lion, Lion, Lion, come back," said Captain Tom Charles. He sat in the captain's chair, waiting for the boat he was meeting to respond over the airways.

A captain with this kind of experience, skill, and knowledge to maneuver across the waters, and with the guts to bring back the exceptional and fragile cargo, puts Tom in very big demand. These trips were not for the softhearted. Captain Tom was not only concerned about the safety of his crew on the boat, but he also worried about the families they all left behind. The job is dangerous, and everyone connected directly or indirectly to it was potentially at risk. The only known way out of this business was DEATH. The people Tom worked for were ruthless and had a nasty reputation with people disappearing that wronged them. Anyone with good sense knew better than to piss these people off.

Captain Tom is speaking very loud on the radio.

"Lion, Lion, Lion, are you there."

Still, radio silence, which made Captain Tom very nervous, when one of the crew members entered the wheelhouse and stated, "We have been sitting here on the edge of the Yucatan Peninsula, waiting for two days now. Captain, how long do you think it will take? The crew is getting a little stir crazy."

"Just do your job, and don't question me. We will be home soon enough," Captain Tom responded.

"Well, Captain, Justin likes to drink, and he is about out of booze. You know how he gets."

"Oh crap!" Captain Tom spouted. "Do we have to deal with this crap every time we come out here?"

"Justin is a bad alcoholic, and we can't figure out why you always bring him on these big jobs."

"He has to earn money just like we do. He has a family, so shut your mouth and stop questioning me. Find something for him now. Whatever it takes to calm him down. I'm sure someone has something on this boat he can take."

Just as Captain Tom looked out of the boat's front window, he could see a large shadow off in the distance approaching them. Captain Tom picked up the binoculars and confirmed what he thought he was seeing.

"Okay, guys, get ready. It's game time."

As they waited, a large freighter was heading straight for them. It was finally close enough to see a particular flag that went up, so Captain Tom knew it was safe to approach and pull up alongside the mother ship. Most freighters could have up to two boats offloading from them at any given time. Then Captain Tom yelled at them, "Hello, Louis. Cómo estás!"

"Hola, Tom. Bien, bien. Can I come aboard and speak to you?"

"Yes, Louis, please come aboard."

Tom knew this had to be important because it took a lot to get from a large freighter to a smaller boat like this one. The ship has a crane that they use to move the drugs from one vessel to another. This time, Louis and his men used the crane to come on board the Star Gazer. As Louis jumped onto the Star Gazer deck, two gunmen came aboard with him, armed and holding their

AK-47s, making them visible to the captain and crew.

"Is everything okay?"

"Yes, everyone is just a little on edge, and they want to be extra careful."

"Okay." Tom asked, "Then what can I do for you?"

"Yes, everything is great. I want you to know we have a little extra on board."

"Extra?"

"Yes, extra. We concluded the deal after you left the dock," Louis said, "and we didn't want to talk about it over the airways."

"How much extra are we talking about?"

"Another six thousand pounds."

"Holy cow, that's a lot extra, all right."

"Can your boat handle the extra weight?"

"Yes, we can handle it, but I don't like it. This will slow us down. I had no idea of the extra cargo."

Louis replied, "Well, the deal is done, and you are to carry the cargo back with you. Your same fees will be paid to you with a little bonus added at the end for your inconvenience."

"Okay, well, we are here, so let's get this below deck and get a move on now."

The guards watched everything the men did, showing their guns to make sure they had no bundle problems. Every bundle has a corresponding number matching the people in Miami. Every package was counted and confirmed to make sure all the numbers matched, and everyone agreed with what came on board before they left the freighter.

"Before we have company in the distance, get the spotter plane up in the air, and start tracking our path home to avoid the traffic."

"What do we have in total today, *amigo*?"

"Eighteen thousand pounds of the pure mother of pearl cocaine."

"Oh hell, then we better get going quick."

The boat has a particular place to stack the special cargo. The vessel has a large live well that would hold live fish that they would catch and carry in until they reach the dock and sell them. The fresher the fish, the better the price they get, but on the bottom of the live well was a hatch hidden deep inside, undetectable and airtight, very small to start with. But once it was open and in full view, you can see just how far and deep space went beneath the deck.

"Okay, it's open now."

A crane took a large cargo net and filled it with the large bales of marijuana that housed the cocaine in their inner core and was moved and placed on the boat deck as the men made a human cargo line to get the drugs below before they could be seen. There was a particular airtight hiding place that was designed just for this type of freight.

"Make sure you stack it tight. Everything has to fit."

As soon as the crew finished loading the fragile cargo, the captain started filling the live well on the boat with water. He told the team to chum the water, get the poles in, and start catching some fish to fill it up.

"We don't want to look suspicious. This way, if they stop us and want to inspect the well, they will have a hell of a hard time getting access to our drugs."

After about an hour, they caught enough fish to fill and load the live well, and Captain Tom told the crew to pull the lines and get ready to ride.

The Star Gazer was a unique boat built with all the latest gadgets available to the fishing industry and then some. Housing two large twin-turbo 1292 diesel engines that were so powerful that it felt as though the Star Gazer would rise out of the water and help her to plane, leaving the smallest amount of foam disappearing as if no boat had ever been there.

Captain Tom knew with the extra weight from the extra cargo they were carrying, and it would cause the boat to go at a little bit of a slower speed, which means it is going to add more time to their trip. Plus, it could add more time to a jail sentence if they get caught. They had to get moving and take the extra precautions that they needed for their safety.

"First, let's get the spotter planes up in the air to map the safest route that we could find to get this load in."

The US Coast Guard Navy had a radio and a radarman who was on their payroll for any job Tom and his crew did. He would report back to the spotter plane on any traffic that they could see on the radar that might cause problems. The US Navy uses the same routes to map and monitor the ships and the traffic in international waters, so it was easy to send the exact coordinates to the spotter plane.

"Mickey, our radarman, had not detected anything unusual so far, so our passage was chosen for us, making sure we have a clear and safe return. Free from anyone."

"Skipper, you are all clear," said a booming voice over the radio.

The pilot from the spotter plane above said, "You have a straight shot to the Marquises, repeat a clear and beautiful moon, no sharks biting tonight."

Captain Tom immediately said, "Let's get moving now."

Once in that area, he knew the smaller boats were waiting for them to drop the drugs. The crew was ready and set up to meet them as quickly as possible.

Captain Tom hit it, full throttle.

Upon arriving in the area, Tom could see some lights blinking off and on in the distance. As they got closer, it was a smaller boat that was set up to meet them. Let's get the water pumped out of the well and start offloading. The big vessel had several drops for the smaller boats to pick up at different destinations. They used a small boat called a T-Craft. The boat's design was unique with a flat bottom and a full width to run at high-speed rates across the flats and shallows where larger ships like the Coast Guard cutters couldn't go.

"Group three thousand pounds per bowie, and make sure everything is airtight, and each has a GPS attached to it."

The coordinates have been given to each of the captains on the boats. Everyone had their designated area to bring the drugs ashore. Some would go north, some would go west, and some would go further north; it depended on the location the cargo was picked up from. The smaller boats would pick up from the water with their coordinates, and then, at a rapid rate of speed, bring the load to another designated area to come ashore. These boats would run through the Ten Thousand Islands off the Everglades, just like it was their playground, and only the local people who were born and raised in that area of the Everglades knew how to maneuver the waters and knew the backcountry like the local boys did.

Once the smaller boat was on approach to bring their cargo ashore, it would be offloaded onto the waiting vans parked in various locations. Local sexy ladies were hired and waiting to drive the goods to different Miami locations. Once in Miami, they would leave the van so that the Columbian partners could pick the van up and offload the drugs for their organization. Then they would return the van to the same spot for the ladies to drive home that same afternoon after a typical day of shopping. Except with a big payday, they were carrying back to the head of the group they worked for.

There were several more drops to make before Captain Tom could bring the big boat ashore. One of the rituals performed on the boats was to wash down the deck with bleach and make sure no residue was left anywhere on it that could incriminate them in any way.

Just as the crew was finishing up the final drop tagging the cargo and throwing it overboard with the GPS attached. The crew started cleaning the boat deck. Captain Tom noticed that Justin was acting a little crazier than usual. He was running around, screaming, shaking, and telling people on the boat that he was going to the authorities as soon as they got ashore, and it was starting to jeopardize the whole trip. Captain Tom noticed the crew was very upset with Justin, and just as one crew member grabbed him, he fainted. Justin started quivering and shaking all over, and then foam began to run out of his mouth. The crew was trying to hold him down and clear his throat, but it was impossible. Justin's strength was far superior to the guys trying to hold him. It was as if he was fighting them every step of the way. Justin got to his knees and took a knife out of his pocket and started to swing it in the air at everyone who came close to him. Before Captain Tom could intervene, one of the crew members took the knife away from Justin and sliced his throat from ear to ear, almost decapitating him. Upon completing the unpleasant task, he then picked up Justin's body holding his head and threw it overboard.

"Now the problem is solved," said JT, one of the crew members.

Tom and the rest of the crew rushed over to the side of the boat. As they stared into the dark, cold, colorless water, all they could see were fish and sharks having a feast on what was visible of Justin's bloody body. The only upside to this was Justin was dead before he hit the water. There was no possible way he could have survived that attack.

This area is known as the Shark River for a reason, and some biggest sharks live and lurk in these waters. Many tales from the older fishermen talk about how dangerous this area is because of the sharks they had encountered. They talk about how they lost their entire catch and nets to some of the giant sharks known to patrol and hunt in these waters that had never been seen to man.

Captain Tom was pissed, and he yelled, "What the HELL! That was uncalled for! We don't do that to each other. We are a team."

Captain Tom looked at the crew and told them to get the bloody mess on the deck cleaned up now. There is no room for error. This now turns from a possible drug charge to a murder charge, and if convicted, the state of Florida carries the death penalty.

"So this is now our little secret and is never spoken of again. The boat has to look as though no one had ever been on it. Use bleach on the deck. How in the hell are we going to explain this to his family?"

Just as the crew finished their cleanup and were heading back to the dock upon the approach to Boot Key in Marathon, the Coast Guard was sitting there waiting for them. With blue lights flashing and over the loudspeaker, the Coast Guard commanded Captain Tom to slow the boat and keep the engines going in a forward motion.

"This is the US Coast Guard cutter, the big *D* of the sea, and we will board your vessel."

Captain Tom did what they asked. He slowed and told the crew to be cool and let them do their job. Just as he instructed the team to come out and stand on deck, the Coast Guard zodiac boat pulled up alongside them with guns drawn and boarded. Once onboard, the zodiac retreated to the cutter, and the men on deck of the cutter held the boat at gunpoint as their captain asked to speak to Captain Tom.

"Do you mind if we look around?"

"Not at all," said Captain Tom. "Do you want to do this at the dock? I have dock space right there."

"No," said the Coast Guard captain. "Keep the boat idle, and I'll come to the wheelhouse. While my guys go and start their search on the boat, why don't you show me all your paperwork so I can make sure you are running this boat legally?"

"Please, be my guest," Tom said.

Captain Tom had the officer come up to the boat's wheelhouse to pull his paperwork from under the counter where he commands the vessel.

"Here is my paperwork, and it's all up-to-date. The guys can show you all the bells and whistles we have onboard for safety."

The Coast Guard crew members started searching the boat, and they made all of Captain Tom's crew come on deck and stay in one spot so they could watch them. It was late afternoon, and as the evening started to set in, they were still in the process of searching the boat. Three hours had passed, but they did not come up with anything, not even a small amount of residue. Captain Tom was beginning to get a little frustrated

"Are we done yet? I would like to go home. We are tired."

"I'll let you know when we are done! Where are you coming from?"

Captain Tom answered, "We have been out all night with not much luck of a catch and would like to end this night with some good sleep."

"Now that you mentioned that, where is your catch?"

"We had no luck. The boat broke down, and we never made it to the fishing grounds, so we just limped back in on one engine."

"Oh, I see," the Coast Guard captain said. "Let's wrap this up. We are going to let you go this time, but so that you know, we are watching you. I don't know how or when or where, but eventually, I will catch your ass, and I will take great pleasure in nailing it to the wall of a jail cell. Good day, Captain Tom," and he threw all his paperwork on the floor of the wheelhouse. And as quickly as they boarded the boat, they exited the boat and retreated on the zodiac that took them back to the cutter as soon as they were on board. They took off and left the captain and crew standing there.

Captain Tom, breathing a big sigh of relief, said, "Let's get this boat to the docks and get out of here before they change their minds."

CHAPTER 3

Coco Plum Beach

It was a beautiful afternoon. The water was crystal clear and no sign of a breeze anywhere. The water was smooth and slick. The beach was clear of all tourists who usually seem to plant their butts in chairs and not move for hours. Tom and his son Jacob decided to take Luke, a two-year-old black Labrador, to the beach for an afternoon of fun and excitement. Jacob is from a previous marriage, and his visitation is every other weekend, and Tom felt, as though with the stress of his job, he needed a little rest to unwind before the next trip. Tom's trip to the beach is a week-end ritual.

"I love the water and this beach. There is no other place like it."

Tom knew this visit was the only one-on-one time he gets with Jacob, and he valued it highly. As they walked the beach, they loved to find old drift-wood pieces and throw them into the water for Luke to chase and retrieve.

Tom had done this several times, and he told his son this is the last one they need to start heading home since they had been gone all day. Just as Tom said that he threw the stick for the last time, Luke did not bring it back. Instead, the dog started barking at a hol-low tree that had blown down and was in the water. It looked like a tree had a limb attached, and it was buried in the sand with the swells of boats passing by; hitting it seemed to dig it in more. Tom called Luke time and time again, but he would not come. He whistled and called back to where the dog was standing. Still no luck. Tom then told his son it would be just like that dog not wanting to go home yet and make him go for a swim to get him.

As Tom swam out to the sandbar and got a little closer, he could see there was something tangled up with the tree. By this time, the dog was going crazy. When Tom stood up, he pulled the tree to see what the heck was making the dog act like that. When he did, he fell backward in the water and was in complete shock to see what partially came up out of the water with the tree. To Tom's amazement, when he rolled the tree over, out popped a piece of Justin's torso from beneath the tree. Tom's heart just sank as he fell backward. The currents had carried the body a long way, and every little and big nibbler of the sea had taken their part of him. It made

Tom sick to his stomach to keep looking at the mangled mess.

Tom called out to Jacob and instructed him to contact the police. Jacob is a typical and curious young man, and he started asking his dad many questions. Tom then yelled back and told Jacob, "Stay on the beach and do what I said and call the police and be quiet." Jacob did as he was asked and placed the call. Jacob could tell by the tone in his dad's voice that it was something terrible.

As the police arrived, Tom was standing back on the beach with Jacob. He had explained that he had just been walking and playing with their dog. When the unleashed dog playing in the surf found the gruesome body, the cops asked Tom to take them back through it step by step and explain what had happened. He then told the police he had no idea who that is in the water.

As Tom finished with their questions, a helicopter swept in and flew low and close to the area. The officer told Tom they were searching the area to see if any other body parts or anything else was visible from the sky. The helicopter flew over and tracked the beach's length and flew back and forth over a square they mapped out, thinking this would be the path the body had taken. Every inch of the area was searched until they were satisfied with their findings.

Since the discovery of the torso, officers representing several law enforcement agencies had converged onto the scene. The colored lights blinked on and off on the underside of the search and rescue helicopter as the low clouds have now started to set in, causing it to turn into an overcast and gloomy late afternoon day. Tom has now decided to turn his attention to the investigation.

The officer handling the investigation said it looked like the deceased was washed in with the early morning tides. Tom knew the body part's identity because of a tattoo on the body's chest area. Justin had just got it put on just a few days before they left on the last job and was very proud of going through the pain and the whole ordeal. Justin had shown it off to him and the crew several times before the trip. Tom could see it was Justin but did not want to alert the authorities because he knew him and knew how he died.

The police took Tom's statement and let him get back to his family. Tom told his son he had enough pleasure for one day and wanted to go home. As Tom and his son were leaving the beach area, the coroner drove up with the all-too-familiar body bag in tow. Tom thought to himself he was glad he was getting his son away from all of that. He didn't want him to see the mess.

Once home, Tom sat on the living room couch and was deep in thought when Jacob approached him.

"What's the matter. You seem sad since we got home."

"Jacob, I am just upset at what we found on the beach."

"Do you think it was a shark that ate the man?"

Tom thought to himself, *Would Jacob still love me if he knew the real story behind that body? Would he understand that what I do is for them, not just myself? These are some of my biggest fears about being caught. Not only would I stand a chance of losing part of my life by going to jail, but I stand a big chance at losing my family for the rest of my life because they disagree with what I have done.*

These were the worries every captain and crew had when they enter this line of work.

Tom finished his beer and popped the top on another one. Tom thought to himself, *And this is going to be a long night. I can't get the image of Justin out of my head, and I feel so guilty about what happened to him because it was on my boat, and he trusted me.*

CHAPTER 4

The Investigation

Two days later, Tom was at the docks in Everglades City, checking out the boats for the next job. Just as he stepped on the deck, two law enforcement officers approached and asked if they could have a minute of his time to ask him some questions.

"Sure," Tom said. "How can I help you?"

"My name is Mark Dean, and this is my partner, John Gonzalez."

"Nice to meet you now, how can I help you?"

"We are investigating a missing person report, and we think you were the last to see him alive."

"Okay, Tom replied. "Who is missing?"

"Justin Thompson. Do you know him?"

Tom's heart sank; he knew this day would come.

"Yes," Tom replied, "he has worked for me from time to time."

"When is the last time you saw him?"

Tom said, "I think about a week or so ago. He came to the boat to see if I had any work for him. He was drunker than I had ever seen him before. You see, Justin is a terrible alcoholic, and he has a terrible time functioning without his booze. I didn't let him work that day. He was too far out of it. He could hardly talk or walk. It is just too dangerous to put someone on the boat like that. I have other crew members I have to protect and keep safe. Justin was a little mad at me, but he just left, and I have not seen him since."

Investigator Mark replied, "But you have seen him."

"Really, where? Because I don't know about seeing him after that?"

"The body that you found on the beach."

"What about the body that I found?"

The investigator responded, "That was Justin."

"Holy shit, I did not recognize him." Tom replied again, "I have not seen him except for the day at the dock."

"Are you sure nothing since then?"

Tom held his breath and said, "No, I am sure. I had no fucking idea."

"Remember, the body had no head, and a lot of it was missing."

"Who in the world would want to hurt Justin like that? I wish I could have helped you more, but that is all I know."

Investigator Mark Dean looked at Tom and wanted to say he was a liar, but instead, he then handed Tom his card and then said, "Well, if there is anything else you can think of, please give me a call and stay close in case we need to speak to you again."

Chapter 5

///

Everglades City, Florida

Everglades City is a small sleepy fishing village with an island attached to it called Chokoloskee. The town sits on some of the most dangerous and exotic terrains on the North American continent. It is surrounded by the great saw grass prairies of the Everglades. Big Cypress Swamp is to the north, and the west is the infamous Ten Thousand Islands. Located in the middle of the Everglades National Park, the islands are magnificent and treacherous to maneuver. The Ten Thousand Islands are scattered with beautiful green mangroves that lead through dozens of tricky passes and unmarked channels that lead to the Gulf of Mexico. Now this area is a haven for fishing. Commercial fishing is the industry of choice with one of the largest fisheries located within the area, making an excellent cover for the new sector lurking on the horizon.

One way in this small village and one way out. Home to about six hundred people who once spent their life commercial fishing for a living. Crab and lobster boats would go out and bring in the catch of the day. This was the primary source of income for the people of this small village. For years, they fished this water and supplied some of the largest restaurant chains with their crab meat and claws to be served to their customers that evening. Different seasons dictate what the fishermen would be out catching. Part of the year was dedicated to net fishing, and it was whatever fish that was in season at that time. A big part of what the locals fished for was king mackerel, mullet, and pompano, to name a few of the fish of choice.

The people lived in older homes most in need of repair, and they drove older rust-bucket trucks to get around town. Most are modest people who did not need much to survive or to be happy. A tight-knit community: most related to each other and did not like outsiders. Defiance and adversity do have a certain appeal. There is a healthy Everglades attitude. If the town's essential character is lawless and defiant, then Everglades City came by it honestly. Given the local history, there is no reason to doubt that drug smuggling lures would easily seduce the townspeople into the trade. Soon, the town would learn this was all about to change and become a reality.

This little village was the central vein for smuggling the drugs into the United States. Large quantities traveled through these dense mangrove swamps from the Gulf of Mexico and other countries. This area is a very harsh environment. Most people wouldn't know the area unless they were born and raised and taught by their forefathers. Some attempted the waterways and never made it back to be seen again.

Drones of mosquitoes would eat you alive, mainly if you were not used to the invasion that happens every year. People who live here have become used to the pesky insects, but when fresh new blood comes into town, it is a full-on assault. Most people would have to use scarves or whatever they have handy to keep them out of their mouths and ears. Some say this would be the last time they would enter this area and never come back again.

This was part of what makes this area so desirable for the drug-running business. The Park Rangers were not familiar with the area and didn't know how to run through the shallow waterways. The bugs and mosquitoes were just a bonus for helping keep outsiders out of the central vein that trafficked most of the drugs into the United States. The fewer people who know the area, the better. There was only a handful of locals that could pull this off. The islands were harsh and unforgiving. One slip up, and it had you either swimming ashore, or you could be a sitting duck on top of the water waiting for help.

CHAPTER 6

Captain Billy T

In a small modest home in the Leigh Cypress area, which is located north of the intersection of Highway 41 and State Road 29 near Carnes Town. This community is known to be a part of the Naples and Marco Island metropolitan area. In this small area lived a man known as Captain Billy, an outstanding fisherman by trade and known as a legend in this area for his ability to be at the right place at the right time to catch some of the bigger loads of fish brought ashore. Still, in the off-season, Billy showed off his real talent as a master carpenter and craftsman building custom boats. Billy was larger than life, but he was one not to play with or piss off. Most people knew that Billy likes to drink, and with the drinking came a temperament that included fighting. And at six feet six and a sturdy square box of solid muscle mass that fit his body frame, you didn't want to get on his bad side.

With a considerable reputation as a local fisherman who fished the waters from the Everglades to the Florida Keys, most people respected him. Still, his true calling was building custom boats with specific designs in them. Billy made it very clear from the start that he would build whatever the people needed, but he would not run any boats or go out and bring any drugs a shorter for anyone. With his talents and craftsmanship, Billy knew he could help give the leading players that brought the drugs ashore an upper hand to make some of the fastest and well-built boats around. Even people from other parts of the world would contract with him to build their commercial fishing boats— some with individual compartments and some without. Most had high-end amenities as some of the most beautiful yachts in the world. This style of boat was designed to be lived on for months at a time if need-be. The handcrafts-manship was superb, and most come with exceptional amenities and equip-ment you would only dream of hav-ing on their boat, and with that came substantial price tags attached to each of them. Billy's reputation was widely known. He would build boats with a special compartment or two in them that was completely undetectable. Only the person who put them in knew how to access them. This put Billy in signif-icant demand to build these boats for the people working the particular trade that entered the area waters where he lived.

Billy owned a large piece of private property located in the middle of the Everglades swamplands, and that is where the magic happened and where these boats came to life. He built a significant portion of them on dry land. Then he would move them to certain areas on the water before completion. Billy would move the boats up and down the coast of Florida, never two in the same spot to keep people from looking at what he was doing, and so no questions could ever be asked.

All monies paid to Billy were in cash, and he would wash it through his company to purchase what he needed to complete the build. Once the hull was crafted and the deck fiberglassed in, he could order the engines, move the boat to any water location available to him, and wait to install them. Most of the machines were exceptional and equivalent to what the coast guard used, especially for speed. The boats are built to outrun anything in these waters. Billy had a reputation for creating some of the fastest boats available in these waters to date. Twin-engine turbo marine diesel was his engine of choice. He spent months building these boats out, and some could take up to a full year to construct, with the specific design and individual needs to be added or implemented into the boat.

Billy was playing around with the design of his boats and came up with an idea. One, he knew he would have to sell to the guys he worked closely with for years. The design was completely different from anything he had designed before. Billy called this boat a go-fast model. It was thirty-two to thirty-eight feet long and all fiberglass with a skinny pointed nose and a square back to help provide stability for the boat. Long and thin, this boat would be packed full of powerful engines, and the fiberglass and shape of the boat made them very difficult to track on radar. The longer and the skinner the boat, the Coast Guard couldn't determine if they were looking at a wave or a boat on the radar, and that means to hit the gas and go as fast as it could go. The long thin needlelike design allowed the cargo to be stacked in the bow of the boat. It is designed with a needlelike sharp nose. This design would allow the boat's nose to punch through the waves like a bullet instead of rolling over the top like a regular boat, making this one of the fastest boats on the water to date.

"The Coast Guard would play hell catching you guys in this." Billy laughed.

Billy estimated this boat could easily do fifty-five to sixty miles an hour in heavy seas. One trip on the regular boat would take four days; now, we have cut that down to two days tops with less crew. Billy was proud of his new design and could not wait to get started on the build. He estimated twelve to eighteen thousand pounds of any type of cargo could be easily stacked in the bow and brought over in one trip, making this one of the most lucrative hauls ever to happen in these waters with just four boats.

The newly built boats and their potential to make this business extraordinarily successful could make the projected profits higher than anyone could have ever expected. Some captains and crews were more successful than others, making some crews mad jealous of the other's success.

Other crews were very competitive and didn't like that they were always being stopped and searched. The captain of other crews would call the Coast

Guard and let them know where and when their competitor's job was happening, so it would send the heat in that direction and allow the captain placing the call to get his load ashore with no hassle. This became an all for one and cutthroat business.

Now Miami's bosses are intrigued and calculating how many extra jobs they could get in with the new equipment and how it was worth the investment. They teased Billy and the captains about how they are indispensable they are becoming to the cartel and how the cartel was going to need even more boats if this worked out.

CHAPTER 7

The Toga Party

Cocaine was the drug of choice to haul or used to party. Through the night, if you drank, you could drink double the amount you usually did, and you could stay up all night, and let's say the ladies of the night enjoyed the sex and endurance that came along with it. The feeling of euphoria was fantastic.

Anytime the team came ashore, the celebration was soon to follow. Being pent-up on that boat for a week or so was nerve-wracking, and the team always felt the need to blow off a little steam once ashore.

Tonight was no exception. The crew partied like there was no tomorrow, and this was a celebration of the job well done and complete, and it didn't hurt that there was an abundance of money and drugs available to all of the men involved.

This job started like any other job, except it was a smaller load. Captain Tom was heading back when they came upon another captain and a crew doing a different job. They were broken down dead in the water, just drifting. Captain Tom navigated the waters with a smaller boat called the Barbara Ann. Tom pulled up alongside them and told the crew to throw them a line to tie them off, and they would tow them in.

When the captain of the other boat called out and said, "I can't do that. I am loaded."

Tom then asked, "With what?"

"With some of the unique cargo that we all carry."

Captain Tom then said, "How much are you carrying?"

"Fifteen thousand pounds."

Captain Tom responded, "You are lucky. I can carry it for you."

Tom's reputation was well-known throughout the Keys and Everglades. The other captain knew the load would be in excellent hands.

"Tell me the location, and I will drop it off for you."

The crew then busted their butts as fast as possible so the drugs could be moved from their boat to the Barbara Ann. The captains traded the coordinates and information for the drop.

Captain Tom asked, "Do you have the other boats set to meet this load?"

He responded, "Yes, I did, but I don't think so now."

Tom said, "I have a good crew who will help you out. Let me contact them."

Tom got on his special radio and asked for Captain Kent and his crew to meet him at the designated location.

Captain Tom then told the other captain, "Do you have someone coming to help you?"

He responded, "Yes, they are on their way."

Just as Captain Tom left the area when he saw the other boat heading in that direction, Tom knew the boat was heading to help them. He saw the towboat tie her off and tow her in on their hip for less visibility, and they were getting out of the area as quickly as they could.

As they were coming ashore, after they had finished all the drops, Captain Tom told his first mate, "Well, we started with a quick job and finished with a big boom. Let's go home."

As they were clearing out the boat of all the supplies and refueling her, a strange man approached them at the dock. Tom was familiar with a Columbian man, but they didn't work for him until tonight.

"Can I have a word with you?"

"Yes," Tom responded. "What can I do for you?"

The man responded by saying, "My boss is very pleased with you, and he wants to show you his gratitude."

"How does he plan on doing that?"

"Well, we are going to celebrate and thank you for getting us out of a tight spot. We are having a toga party in your honor. Here is the address in Miami. You guys come and bring the crew. We will cover all expenses."

Captain Tom responded, "We will be there."

Pablo Escobar was a Colombian man with a fearsome reputation on the streets of Medellin, Columbia. Pablo was a self-made millionaire who built his gang to control the importing of marijuana and cocaine into America and bring prosperity back to Columbia. Pablo was the underling of a powerful kingpin of the Medellin Cartel. He had a combination of intelligence and street smarts, which enabled him to rise above all competitors. Some people who sought his advice gave in and joined his gang. Those who felt nervous and frustrated felt safe in his company working for him rather than against him. He earned their respect by remaining calm in hazardous situations. Some feel he is a man with a mighty aura. With this type of reputation, Pablo made many enemies. No one could get next to Pablo Escobar without encountering a bodyguard or two. When he traveled into Miami, it was rare to see Pablo; only a select few could meet with him. Everyone else had to meet with his associate who he sent in his place. But make no mistake, Pablo Escobar was who they all worked for.

Tom and two of the crew headed to Miami, and the party had already started. These guys could drink like fish and could go all night long. As they arrived in Miami, they met up with the Miami contacts at a bar, and they followed the Columbian men to a condo complex and led them to the top floor, "the penthouse." The elevator was private, and it only opens to the penthouse. The guys stepped off the elevator in amazement at what they were seeing. This very massive man started to approach them. He was clean-cut and well-dressed, jewelry adorned tastefully, and walked with someone in charge with a superior attitude—the head of the cartel, Pablo Escabor's right-hand man Mario Gonzalez.

The guys were greeted, and then the ladies escorted them to the seats in the living area. As they entered the room, one particular lady was lying on a coffee table nude. Another woman started passing out small mirrors of cocaine for each of them and their drink of choice. Mario told the men they are here to enjoy themselves. As he walked up to the table, he said, "Captain Tom, this lady I handpicked her and two others just for you."

Tom looked down and saw one of the most beautiful women he had ever laid eyes on. She was perfectly portioned for the frame of her body. Tom started to get aroused just by looking when Mario took a spoon of his cocaine from his bag and placed a generous amount on top of the young woman's clitoris for Tom to lick off. Tom definitely did as he was told, and the young woman moaned in pleasure. Tom looked down and saw his body responding positively to what he was tasting and looking at the young woman's body.

Tom then took her and the two other women to one of the bedrooms that had been set up for them. As Tom entered the room, the ladies had already started to disrobe him. First his shoes, then his shirt, and then his pants; all the while, Tom had his hands full playing with his new playmates. Tom reached under one of the ladies' dresses to find she had nothing on underneath it. She was wet and sweet and ready. Tom could not get into the bed quick enough. He laid on his back while one started stroking him until he was fully engulfed when he looked up and saw another starting to place herself on his face. Each woman took turns with Tom, while the other two were going down on each other for him to watch. The sex was wet, wild, and kinky and lasted all night. After a couple of hours of taking turns, Tom decided he needed a shower. Each of them entered the shower with him and washed him from head to toe.

After Tom and the ladies exited the main room, Mario ensured the other two men they would be treated with the same pleasures. Just as they began to do their usual snorting of the infamous drug, Mario approached the men and told them how grateful he was to them for what they had done and how it did not go unnoticed. The first of the crew, Arthur, was then asked to follow him to another room. Arthur, who is eager to get started, said, "Let's get this party started."

His clothes were partly off before they got to the room. The guest suite was set up to accommodate him and the two women that were waiting on the bed for him to arrive with nothing on but their birthday suits. Each opened their legs wide so they could show Arthur what they were about to give him. Just as they saw him looking and licking his lips, one of the girls rolled over on her knees and put herself in the air and then started working on the other girl, teasing her until she was brought to a full climax. She then opened herself wide to show him she was ready to be taken. Arthur couldn't pass on the chance to pleasure her and watch her work on the other girl. Then he smiled as the third placed herself on the girl's face that was lying on her back. Arthur was in heaven. Every ten minutes or so, they would switch positions to start again.

Meanwhile, Kent was waiting on the couch with one of the ladies lying on her back in her panties. The women started to unbuckle his pants while they were waiting for Mario to return, and the favorite special of the night was the art of fellatio. Kent could not help but love it. After she completed the task at hand, and since Mario was taking a little longer than usual, she stripped off her panties and asked him to take her right there. She asked Kent if he wanted a taste as she placed the cocaine in all of her sweet spots for him to lick off. Kent yelled, "Hell yes," and got on his knees and was experiencing pure erotic pleasure. He worked his tongue in and out and all over the young woman's female parts until he had her just where he wanted her. She was begging him to make love to her, and then Kent plunged himself deep inside her hot, wet, moist box until she was screaming in erotic pleasure, reaching her climax.

Mario then returned for Kent, and he looked at them and said, "I could see you guys have already started." The other two women stopped Kent and took him by his hand and began escorting him to the third suite for their full night of provocative and uninhibited anything-goes sex and a night of pure pleasure. Each girl had a specialty they enjoyed. All of the girls loved to be played with at the same time. Kent took on the challenge and fulfilled his job making these women extremely satisfied and happy for the night.

Morning came way too soon. All the men were sluggish and hungover and whipped from the night of passion with the women. Kent looked at Tom and said, "I feel like someone beat the shit out of me."

Tom looked at him and said, "You look like someone beat the shit out of you."

Breakfast was now served on the Lani. Only Tom was asked to join Mario in his private dining room. Once inside, Mario told Tom, "You look terrible, you need a bump to get you going?"

Tom replied, "No, I'm okay. I just need coffee to get me awake."

Mario said, laughing, "You are going to need a bucketful. I need you to pay attention so we can talk about the next job."

Tom asked, "What do you have in mind?"

Mario replied, "We have a large load that needs to be picked up off the Yucatan Peninsula."

"What's the load?"

"Marijuana with a little cocaine. The freighter carrying the drugs will be called the 'Blue Runner,' and she would be carrying thirty thousand pounds of marijuana plus cocaine. This job will be one of the largest loads ever to be done in these waters. If we can pull this off, it will be a new milestone for the guys I work with."

"Okay, we can handle that. It is going to take some planning, and the timing has to be perfect. When do we need to be out on the water?"

"Tonight, here are your coordinates. You are the best in the area with the best reputation of not getting caught, and it has been a little hot out there. I need someone I can trust."

Tom sat for a few minutes and picked at breakfast and looked at Mario and said, "Thank you for the hospitality and an unforgettable evening. We better get going if we are going to get everything ready for this job."

Tom then asked Mario, "One thing, the drop that is scheduled for tonight needs to happen in a week, so I can make sure we are ready. It is rough out there right now, and for this large of a load, we are going to need a lot of extra help."

Mario replied, "Okay, I will give you the extra days, and I will talk to them and get it changed."

"Who is my point of contact?"

"Louis, like always." Tom stopped and stared with a blank face looking at Mario. Mario then laughed and looked back at Tom and said, "Didn't you know pretty much everyone eventually works for me?"

CHAPTER 8

Cozumel, Mexico

Riding off into the sun brought another day of beautiful weather for now. The Star Gazer with Captain Tom at the helm once again en route to meet the freighter off the Yucatan Peninsula.

This trip was not going to be so lovely and smooth. As the Star Gazer got closer to the Yucatan Peninsula, the water began to get choppy, and the wind started to pick up. The clouds were already turning dark. The water was cold and rough with the rain and the winds whipping and tossing the boat around.

Times and locations were set. They couldn't be changed now. Tom was extra careful not to trigger off the Coast Guard as they left US waters and began to cross into the Yucatan, but the weather did not disappoint. The wind was now blowing forty-five miles an hour, and it was expected to worsen, and the waves were getting more prominent; this was what Tom had predicted. "The captain told the crew, "Batten down the hatches, boys, it would be a rough ride. Put everything away now, or it would end up as a projectile flying through the air, and god only knew the damage it could cause to the crew or the boat."

Captain Tom was having one hell of a hard time keeping this boat on course. The bow of the boat was going completely underwater and then popping back up again. Waves were crashing over the wheelhouse. Captain Tom looked at his charts, and he could see they were just outside of Cozumel, Mexico, and Cozumel has an excellent harbor for them to take refuge in until the storm passes. It would give him and the crew a chance to check the boat out and make sure nothing happened to it during that rough ride and stretch their legs and go ashore after being tossed around like a Ping-Pong ball on a tennis table. He also needed to contact his partner that he was meeting and let him know there would be a little delay.

"That was always a little scary. I don't want to encounter that weather when we load to go back, or we could lose some cargo or people if our boat sank."

Captain Tom always carried a bag of cash on board for emergencies.

"Well, I think I can classify this as an emergency," Captain Tom said. "We can refuel and anchor out in the harbor and rest. Let me contact our friends and let them know where we are so they can make arrangements for us. Hopefully, the drop-off can be somewhere closer to where we are."

Just about that time, they looked up and saw a Mexican gunboat heading in their direction, and the guns were being handled and pointed straight at them.

"This is not going to be good."

Captain Tom met General Hernandez who has a reputation for being ruthless as he boarded the boat.

"Hola, General."

"Hola, Captain Tom."

"Is that correct?"

"Yes, I am Tom"

"What are you doing in Mexican waters?" The general asked.

"We are having some engine problem and needed to take refuge, so we had to come ashore."

"You Americans always think that you can trash our country with all your drugs."

"No, sir, there are no drugs on the boat."

"I think this boat is going to be mine, and there is not a damn thing you can do to stop me from taking it."

"Please, General, we mean no disrespect. I have a gift for you for allowing us to be here. We would be so grateful may I show you."

"Yes, show me, and don't pull any funny stuff."

"Would you follow me please?"

Captain Tom and the general made their way to the wheelhouse of the boat. Captain Tom told the crew to be calm while he met with the general.

"As you can see, General, here it is." Captain Tom pulled out a cash bag and gave the general 250,000 dollars. "Would that make you happy?"

The general looked at Captain Tom and said, "How do you know that I will not take your money and your boat?"

"Because I work for you, Brother Louis," Captain Tom said. "Yes, General Hernandez, your brother told me about you."

General Hernandez began to laugh out loud. "Well, then you are family. *Mi casa es su casa*." The general then yelled down to the other men, "It's okay, they work with Louis. Let them go and escort them to the best spot on the dock to refuel and restock some food and supplies. Here is your money back. Louis pays me plenty."

The general then looked at Captain Tom and said, "If you need anything, please give me a call. I will contact Louis and let him know you are here. Don't cause any problems on our small island while you are here. I will clear anything you need."

"Okay, thank you, General. I do have a favor."

"Ask."

"I'll have a young lady coming in from south Florida, and she has some equipment that I need to clear customs. If you could please help me out so she can come through without being hassled, I would forever be grateful.

The general responded, "Consider it done."

The morning came, and Captain Tom went to the airport to meet Sara. Sara was a lady who lived with him in the Keys, and she carried a few things over there for him and the boat.

"How was the flight?"

"Great. I'm glad to see you and glad to be here."

"Did you have any problem clearing customs?"

"Not at all. I was waved right through."

"Got to love the general." Tom laughed. "Well, let's go to the hotel and get you settled in."

"Great, I have something special for the captain, if you know what I mean."

"Let's go. I would love to see it."

As Sara and Tom entered the room, they could see it was spectacular: very plush first class all the way. Champagne on ice and strawberries waiting on a tray.

"Wow," Sara responded. "You spared no expense. This is awesome."

"I wish I could take credit for this, but the general set this up. So, Sara, what do you have for me to unwrap?"

She kicked her shoes off and started to untie her dress. "What do you think, Captain, did you miss me?" She then dropped the dress on the floor and stepped out of it. "What do you think of my new bra and panties or the lack of?"

"Oh, I think this is great." As Tom moved closer to her, he bent his head low and covered her lips with his. Her lips clung to his, and she could not have denied that kiss if she wanted to. His whiskers were rough and exciting, her lips were warm and moist, and he worked playfully to part hers. His tongue was darting in and out slow, thoroughly erotic. He skimmed the inner lining of her lips and then plunged his tongue far inside the hollow of her mouth.

"Oh god, Tom, I thought I would die if I didn't get to have you."

Tom's assessment of the wild and erotic feelings he was feeling made him full and erect, and this situation didn't stop him from taking full advantage of her vulnerability. Their mouth fused again, and she marveled over the evocative power he had over her. She felt his kisses all the way through her body to her toes. The tingling swirled around her breast through her belly and then to her thighs. She slid her hand into his pants and was glad to see him fully engulfed and ready to please her.

"Please, please, don't stop now. I want you."

Greedily, her hand began to caress him, and he took the lead with her until she was frantic with need. He became excited, and he could feel how warm she was. He then pushed her down on the bed and made his way down to her panties to reveal a beautiful, warm, wet spot that was so sensitive that she moaned every time he brushed it and kissed it to tease her and get her more excited. Just as he kissed her soft, damp spot, he took two fingers and pushed them hard and deep inside of her, which caused her to cry out in great pleasure.

"Yes! You remember just how I like it, don't you, Tom?"

Tom took his fingers, worked them fast and intensely several times. He took them out, spread her legs, and pushed himself deep inside her.

"Oh god," she cried out in pleasure, "please don't stop. I am about to explode."

Just as she said that, Tom pulled out, and she looked puzzled. "What's wrong? I want you to beg me for it. Oh, please, Tom, you are a bad little boy, and I need you deep inside me, please give it to me now."

Just as she said that, he plunged deep inside of her. Tom worked himself in and out a few times until he felt her explode with pleasure. She grabbed his back and moaned with every stroke he made, and as she climaxed again, he finished as well, bringing their encounter to full erotic pleasure.

Morning came all too quickly as Captain Tom got up to Sara having a bubble bath in the tub for two.

"Do you mind if I join you?"

"Please do, this would be a great way to end our weekend trip."

Tom and Sara made mad passionate love. She loved to let him explore every inch of her body. She would usually let him have his way with her any way he wanted. As they finished round two in the tub, Tom realized what time it was and told Sara, "We have to get moving."

The look on both of their faces was like an agreement that they both knew but never spoke of. Sara knew this could be the last time they ever see each other, and it broke her heart.

"Oh darn, already I wanted round three."

"Round three will have to wait until I get home. Let's get you ready for your flight back, and I will see you at home in a few days, and we can finish where I left off."

"Wow, that was quick, getting rid of me already? You don't want me to hang around for a few more days?"

"No, then I won't be able to keep my mind on work. Besides, we are leaving this afternoon to take the boat back."

He called the front desk and asked them to call a cab to drive Sara to the airport and get him to the harbor. As he got to the airport, he promised Sara it would not be more than a couple of days, and he will be home. He kissed her, took a bracelet off her wrist, and promised to return it when he got there. You see, most fishermen are superstitious and feel if they have something that belongs to someone special in their life, they would be allowed to have a safe passage home and then return it to her. Tom then turned her around and brought her to the desk check-in for the flight home.

The porter knew precisely how to get her back through the customs line. Tom tipped the porter and told him not to let anything happen to her.

The porter responded, "The general gave me strict instructions to make sure she is well taken care of and didn't miss her flight. Tom got back in the cab and waved to Sara as he drove off."

Tom headed to the marina where his boat was anchored in the harbor. He tipped the taxi driver and asked if a boat could take him out to the Star Gazer. People in Mexico are not used to seeing a boat like this. The Star Gazer was too big to stay at the dock, so it had to be anchored away from everyone in the middle of the harbor to guarantee its safety.

"*Si, Capitan Tom*, we have a boat waiting for you. The general said I am to accommodate you with anything you need."

"Great, just get me out there, and we will be on our way."

"Gracias," Captain Tom said as he got up on the Star Gazer and fired up the engines. He gave the boat's engine a once-over, which was a ritual that Tom did before every job.

"De nada and safe travels, amigo."

They loaded the drugs onto the boat in the harbor with the Mexican gunboat standing guard, so they had no problems. The vessel is equipped with another hidden area. The crew pulled the bow of the boat apart and exposed the metal frame.

"What are we going to do with this?"

As the Mexican guards watched, the crew hid ten thousand pounds of cocaine into the boat's interior walls and then welded it shut with no signs of the boat ever being tampered with.

It looked just like it did when it left the dock.

"We leave at 2:00 a.m., our time, no bullshit, we all sleep on the boat. I have already taken Sara back to the airport for her flight back. Be here, or I will leave you."

They looked up and said, "We got it."

"No one gets on this boat. The general will guard it for us until we leave."

It was early morning, and Captain Tom made his way out of his bunk in the wheelhouse.

"Let's get her fired up and warm the engines," Tom informed the crew there had been a lot of traffic out there the last couple of days, and the Mexican gunboats will escort them and get them as close to US waters as they can. "One other thing, this is Jose, and he will be making the trip back with us. Nothing happens to him, do I make myself clear!"

Jose has been embedded with the crew on the boat intentionally. The Columbians were the people they do business with. This was how the Columbians can guarantee what happens to the trip and how successful it was. They monitor the load and report back to the cartel's head man, whether it made it across with or without any problems. Once they arrive safely back, Jose, the Columbian, would contact his people, give them a report, and ask for his plane ticket home.

Just as they crossed into international waters, the spotter plane pilot came into view and went on the radio and said, "Yellowfin, watch your net, the sharks are bad. I just saw a net get eaten up." Immediately, Tom opened the throttle up to full blast, but with the weight of the cargo, he could not maneuver around them or outrun them this time.

Tom got closer to a large shadow that was off in the distance. He could see it was getting closer. It wasn't a Coast Guard vessel. The boat was riding extremely low in the water. As Tom approached the boat, he could see mice jumping off the boat and swimming toward them. Tom knew that it was not a good sign. That is another wise tale from the old fishermen of the sea. The legend goes that if you see a mouse leaving a boat, it usually means the vessel is taking on water and will probably sink. Tom could also see the boat had some cargo on board but didn't know what it was. The other boat then fired two shots across the bow and asked the captain to pull alongside and stop the engines.

"We need to come aboard and to speak to you."

Tom did as they asked. Both boats were rocking and rolling in the choppy waters of the Yucatan. In the hot summer afternoon, when the boat got close enough for them to board, three men jumped on the boat's bow with guns drawn and pointed straight at Tom and the crew.

Tom told the crew to hang tight because he didn't know what was going on, but this was not the law. As Tom slowed the boat, the three men entered the wheelhouse and asked if they had any extra fuel.

Tom explained, "No, they didn't because they only carry enough to go and come." Raul then explained that they have no choice but to take the Star Gazer. He asked, "Can't you call someone to bring you fuel? We do it all the time."

Raul then responded, "You call them for us."

Tom responded, "I would rather not. I'm on a deadline to get back to shore."

Raul was furious and said, "Why, what do you have on this boat?"

Tom responded, "Nothing. I am running empty."

Tom knew if they found the drugs on the boat, it would be a death sentence for him and the crew. Tom also knew they could not say a word, just try to help them as much as possible and get them on their way. Tom then told Raul, "I could call someone for you, but it will take about four to five hours to get them here."

Raul agreed to wait, but they were going to do it with them on the Star Gazer. Tom knew that it was a bad idea, but he went along with it and called for more fuel. Tom then confirmed that the fuel would be there as quick as they could get it, so the distressed boat could be on their way.

"Okay, Raul, your fuel is on the way. Hopefully, it will get here soon."

Tom noticed that Raul's boat was sitting even lower in the water than he expected, and he asked Raul to check it out or it could sink. Raul told Tom, "I want two of your crewmen to go below deck with me and look and see what is wrong."

As the guys got on the boat and went down to the engine room, they could see the boat was taking on water as they had suspected, and it was going to sink if they didn't do something to try and stop it. They told Raul that they needed to turn the bilge pump on and start pumping this water out before it gets too bad. Raul didn't know what that was, but he told them to do what they needed. After about an hour, they finally got the pump to start working, but it was intermittent and did not stay on like it was supposed to. The crew came back to the vessel, the Star Gazer, and told Tom if that fuel did not get there quickly, there was a big chance that the boat could sink, and it was full of drugs. Tom told the crew that it created a big problem because he didn't know if it was going to get here in time or not.

After a couple more hours of fighting and trying to keep the water out of that boat, by the grace of God, the fuel boat finally arrived. Captain Tom told Raul that the calvary came to help them, and they worked for the same people he did, and they would take care of them with their fuel needs. Tom then said to Raul that he needed to get going because he had detained him long enough, and he was running way behind schedule. Raul finally agreed. As Tom and the crew of the Star Gazer pushed off, there was a little uneasy feeling that came over him, but the men with the fuel had said they would be fine and would help and make sure they get all the fuel they needed.

Tom opened up the throttle and started back en route to get his cargo safely ashore.

As Jeff and Andy came on board with Raul, the other men with him started speaking to him in Spanish, and the men had no idea what they were talking about, nor did they care. Raul then looked at Jeff and Andy and said, "My boat is taking on water, and I need your boat."

Jeff told Raul, "We couldn't do that, this isn't our boat."

And before they said anything else, they shot both Jeff and Andy in the head and killed them instantly.

Raul ordered his crew to get the bodies taken care of and clean the boat up quickly. The crew took Jeff and Andy one at a time and wrapped them in a led line from a fishing net that was onboard. Then they secured the bodies to a barrel of fuel after they gutted the men and threw them over the side of the boat, making sure that the bodies had sunk and disappeared to depth unknown. As the crew looked over the side, the men disappeared slowly and went out of sight, never to be seen again.

Raul ordered his crew to hurry up and get the boat cleaned because they would have to move the drugs from their boat to the other boat before their boat sank. After an hour and a half, all of the drugs were moved and stacked on the deck just as they saw the boat listing to the right side with the motor running. Raul then quickly ordered his crew to get on their boat for the last time, remove anything they wanted and or needed before it sank, and then blew a hole in the bottom of it so it would help move it quickly and sink to the bottom of the sea to its final resting place.

CHAPTER 9

Coast Guard
Searching the Boat

As Captain Tom was just about to enter the mouth of Boot Key where the marina was located to dry dock, the Coast Guard cutter, the big *D* of the sea, came into sight. Blue lights were flashing. They came over the loudspeaker and told them to slow the boat so that they could board the vessel. Tom slowed the engines and thought, *Not again. I have had enough of this crap and let them on board.*

The Coast Guard boarded the boat and started a white glove search, which they were so famous for performing as they called it. No drugs were found on the boat while Tom and the crew were detained and held in the scorching sun for hours.

Now as the evening hours approached, they asked again, "Where are the drugs? I know they are on board."

Captain Tom responded, "There isn't anything on the boat, and I don't know what you are talking about. We are getting tired of sitting here and want to leave."

The captain of the Coast Guard yelled at him, "Sit your ass down until I tell you to get up!"

Captain Tom sat back down and watched as they were ripping the boat apart. "Are you kidding me? You can't do this!"

Stuff was flying everywhere. Pots and pans from the kitchen were thrown about in the cabin and on deck. Food, clothes, and personal possessions were dumped onto the floor of the boat.

It was now the early morning of the following day, and the big *D* crew was still on board, and their search came up with nothing. Tom looked at his team and said, "Let them do what they need to do and stay calm!"

After they continued searching the boat for several more hours and found nothing, not even a bottle of baby powder on board, the Coast Guard captain was getting a little upset. He held the crew and Captain Tom for forty-eight more hours, desperately trying to find anything they could use to justify the search and haul the boat back to port. After being harassed and the same question asked repeatedly and about two days into the investigation, they still came up empty. The US captain of the cutter called for backup. To the surprise of the captain, nothing was found during the search. Frustrated, they started to search the crew one at a time. Suddenly, one of the officers said that they hit pay dirt. They found a personal stash, a small amount of marijuana in one of the crewmen's pockets. This gave the Coast Guard the probable cause they needed to confiscate the boat, haul it back to the Coast Guard docks, and do a more in-depth and complete search.

Captain Tom told his crew, "This is bullshit. I don't allow that crap on this boat."

After another day back in port, the Coast Guard let Captain Tom and all the crew go, even the man found with the joint in his pocket. There was not enough evidence to charge him with anything so far, but they would not release the boat back to Tom and the crew. However, to no avail, they still found nothing because the drugs were undetectable and well tucked away in a metal casing that was so well hidden, even with all the resources they had at their disposal. Suddenly, the Coast Guard found a small baggie of pot under the captain's bed.

"Well, look at what we found."

"That's bullshit," Tom said. "I don't smoke pot."

But it gave the Coast Guard the right to confiscate the boat and send it to be auctioned off. They then tagged the boat and waited a week to go to court to get the right to sell her and send it to be sold.

After about six months, the Star Gazer was taken to the Miami River and anchored, waiting for its turn to be placed on the auction block for sale. The auction was large, and the boat will be sold as is and sold to the highest bidder.

Word got out quickly and back to Mario, Tom's connection in Miami. With the boat being placed for auction,

Mario had to move fast and make sure they were the highest bidder to get the boat back for Tom and get the drugs that are still hidden in the boat's wall. The drugs alone had a street value of over five million dollars, and they were still in the boat, and it would be handed over to the new owners upon finalizing the purchase.

The day of the auction was stressful. Waiting to see if they got the boat back without a blood bath in the middle of the Miami streets was one of the hardest things Tom had ever experienced. The Miami Columbian connection was successful in being the top bidder on the boat. The boat's hidden cargo made a little less profit, but the cartel was happy with the return.

Next time, we will have to be a little faster and smarter, thought Tom.

CHAPTER 10

Men Lost at Sea Forever

Now several days had passed, and the men who took the fuel to the other boat still had not come back home or made contact with the boss of the crew they worked for. The first thing that the organization did was send a plane up to search the area of the boats' last coordinates. The aircraft came back empty-handed with no information about the men or boat being found. The crew then asked all of the local fishermen and any pleasure boat going out to keep an eye out for the men and or wreckage of the boat. They were deemed missing.

The US Coast Guard search and rescue team was notified that it had been seventy-two hours and with no sign of the boat or men and with no contact with any of them, nor with any wreckage from the boat recovered. The red flags for a good outcome were far from happening. The townspeople who were involved in this job, from the Florida Keys to the Everglades, were very concerned, and everyone was on high alert. All local fishermen were asked if they were out on the water to please keep an eye out for any wreckage.

Days went by, and the US Coast Guard search and rescue had no choice but to call off the search and declare the probability of the men being found as very slim, and they were all presumed dead. Too much time had passed, and the storms moving through the area didn't give them much of a chance of survival.

The families were devastated: mothers lost sons, wives lost husbands, and children lost their dads since all the men were in their early thirties and should have great life still ahead of them and a chance to live it to the fullest. To date, no bodies nor boats have ever been recovered. This will continue to be one of the unsolved mysteries of the sea.

CHAPTER 11

The Harassment

Not only did Captain Tom and the crew worry about being hijacked by outlaw crews trying to steal the drugs, now the harassment started with the DEA. They chased, followed, and listened to the men they suspected in the area of drug trafficking. They started watching closely in an attempt to catch one of them slipping up. The pressure was a little too tedious for comfort. The DEA was trying to put as much pressure on the locals and the local law enforcement, but little did they know that the area's top smugglers were paying the local law enforcement to look the other way. Word of the new business was all over the small village. People were excited when they learned the amount of money that could have been made from the new business brought in from the outside.

People bought new cars. The Lincoln Continental was the car of choice, and as you drive through the small city, you can see some of the new homes that were recently built. Jewelry of the best kind was bought and worn proudly by some of the community's poorest citizens just a few months ago. The latest fashion designers were a girl's best friend. With the latest fashions available on the market to date, the women became very demanding. Most are trying to outdo the other. The boats, homes, and vehicles were expensive, but they were not the costliest. If this is lavish, you must think that Everglades City must have been truly poor before the drug smuggling started.

All the local people participated in this business one way or another to maintain their lifestyles. People were branching out into hauling all types of drugs since the rumors flowed out about how successful the drug business was. All the local people had to do was not talk to anyone and keep their mouths shut, but that was impossible from an area where everyone knew each other. Everyone always knew each other's business, and most were related.

The drug enforcement agency conducted an investigation on another group of people known as the top smugglers of the area, and the government named the crew the Saltwater Cowboys. The Daniels crew was at the top of the list for indictment. This investigation was ongoing for two years. The code name for this investigation was Operation Everglades. The smugglers knew only to hire local people they knew, but they never thought someone close to them would talk and give up some of the players.

During the investigation, an agent named William J. Segarra masqueraded himself as Willie Santos, a drug smuggler. Unknown to the group at various times, the DEA had agents embedded with him as well to assist.

On a hot summer night, at the invitation of Levi Dupree, Segarra held several meetings to make the arrangements for a shrimp boat to receive thirty thousand pounds of marijuana from a freighter off the Yucatan Peninsula in the Gulf of Mexico and transport it to shore. During the meeting, a discussion of an additional ten thousand pounds of marijuana on a separate load would also be shipped for the five men attending the meeting. M. Wells, J. Charles, M. Richards, R. Janes, and K. Tomlin

were the five men involved with setting this job into motion. On the night
when the job is to take place, little did
the men know that Special Agent Rene
Gonzalez traveled on the Yellowfin from
Panama City in an attempt to establish
communication with the Blue Runner,
the freighter carrying the drugs. The
contact was to happen off the Yucatan.
After failing to establish any connection,
he returned to Panama City. At that
point, the agent had no choice but to
act on the information provided earlier
by agents Pullen and Dupree. He contacted the US Coast Guard to stop and
board the fishing vessel "Barracuda." It
is the boat meeting the freighter called
Blue Runner that is carrying the thirty
thousand pounds of Marijuana.

The Coast Guard, in full pursuit,
chased the fishing vessel that carried the
contraband. The captain gave the order
to throw the job, meaning toss the bales

overboard. After hours of chasing them through the dark and rough waters, the boat was seized, and the contraband and all occupants were transported to Key West to be processed and charged.

Now the local people in the drug smuggling business were running scared, looking at anyone they didn't recognize or know and were new to the area. Rumors were going around town on who the next people were to be arrested. People were now turning themselves in and turning on each other, trying to cut deals before being indicted, making this town a dangerous place to live. The DEA is stepping up the heat on anyone they suspected of smuggling and living or working in the area.

Billy was not a smuggler per se, but he knew enough about the organization's key players that made him a person of interest and one to harass. The antagonizing became more and more. Billy was summoned to appear in front of the grand jury for the state of Florida several times, but there was never enough evidence to indict him. This didn't stop the pressure and the harassment from the DEA. They followed him. And every chance they got during the early morning hours, they would board his boat and search it without Billy's knowledge or permission.

CHAPTER 12

Bogus Charges

Today was a typical day in the Keys, but one of those days, the sheriff probably should not have attempted to contact Billy with the bogus charges they were trying to attach to him. A local law enforcement officer named R. Damsey contacted Billy and asked him to come to the dock where he docked his boat called the Judge. Billy did, and when he got there, they asked him to come on board the boat. Billy knew R. Damsey but did not know the DEA agent. The agent told Billy they needed to show him something. Billy asked them what they were doing on the boat without permission, and they went through the whole routine again, telling him they had a tip that there were drugs on this boat, which gave them probable cause to search it.

Billy became furious and said, "Where are the drugs?"

"This boat has never had any drugs on her and never will."

That is when the DEA agent held out his hand and told Billy they found these two seeds on the boat, and it was evident that the boat had drugs on it. Billy got close and looked at the seeds and then picked them up and threw them in the water and said, "What evidence?"

The DEA agent lunged at Billy and tried to stop him, and that was when Billy made a fist and hit this man so hard that he knocked him down onto the deck of the boat.

Officer Damsey said, "There is my car. Billy, get in the back seat. You are under arrest."

Officer Damsey then told Billy he didn't want any trouble. He had known him for a long time, and he was just doing his job.

Billy looked at Damsey and said, "Maybe it is time for you to get another job because this is bullshit, and you know it."

Everyone knew Billy was not one to tangle with, and if you did, you better have all of your ducks in a row. Billy was arraigned, bail was paid, and back out on the streets the following morning.

The harassment continued, and the pressure was building, getting to be more and more intense. This is where mistakes can be made and throw alcohol and drugs in the mix, and it can put you into a vulnerable state, which can make you move your lips and talk about things that should never be discussed. An old fisherman tale is "loose lips sink ships."

CHAPTER 13

///

The Explosion

The Janes family—a family who had to learn the hard way. This particular family was well-liked and well established within the community. Mr. and Mrs. Janes had seven children. One particular son named Ronnie got himself arrested for doing something stupid without thinking about the job. Ronnie had just gotten out of jail a few months earlier, and now with the new laws changing, he was looking at going away for life. Ronnie was buried in the new drug trade that plagued the area. The DEA had a three-year investigation going on a group of smugglers. The involvement put Ronnie in a challenging position. One was to keep himself out of jail, and the other is to keep his family safe. The government started cracking down on all the drug smugglers trying to bust up the organizations in the area. They believe it was one of the main arteries for the drug business to function.

Ronnie was running scared and had a large loudmouth. His family cautioned him not to say things that could hurt himself or others in the business. Still, Ronnie being the hardheaded type, only worrying about himself and not wanting to go back to jail, didn't listen to anyone. The DEA promised the witness protection program for him and his family after he wore a wire to a couple of meetings with the people he always dealt with in the business. In exchange, he would provide the names of the people he was connected to and worked for in Miami, along with the tapes and any information on any deals that were about to happen.

The Miami organization was ruthless and unsympathetic, heartless, cold, and did not play games. Life was nothing to the person who dares to cross them. They were about money and nothing more.

Ronnie was moved very quickly to another area within the state and was relocated and placed in a safe house. He was allowed to say goodbye to his friends and family before he left. Soon after the goodbyes were said after he did what they had asked and once the family is protected, Ronnie and his family could no longer have any more contact with anyone from their past. As his final friends left the house, the DEA agent moved in. It was now very early in the morning when the streets were silent and bare with no traffic. The time had come for Ronnie and his family to get their new identities. This would be the last time he would get to see the place he grew up in and the last time he would get to use his given name and surname his parents gave him when he was born. This area and the people were what Ronnie knew and grew up with, and he felt a true betrayal that he was forced to do to family and friends. Ronnie also knew the consequences of him not helping the government, and he knew he would be marked as a snitch, and the cartel was sure to place a hit on his and his family's life.

It was early morning, and the village was tranquil and still when the elder of the Janes family, Mr. John Janes, got up and did his morning routine by getting the coffee ready for the family when they got up. He sat quietly, thinking about how nice it was to have all the kids home, even Ronnie. John remembered that Christmas was the last time they had all been together under one roof. Family meant everything to him, and it was all he lived and cared about. John went outside and saw one of his son's trucks parked in the driveway behind his vehicle. Well, he thought it was too early in the morning to wake the others to move the vehicle, so he decided he would drive his son's truck and take it and have it serviced for him in the nearby city of Naples, which was about thirty miles from where they lived. Mr. Janes left the keys to his truck and wrote a note teasing his son about how he was going on a joyride and would be back late in the afternoon and not to wait up on him. If you need to go anywhere, you can use my truck. James was an early bird and always got up at the crack of dawn to help his sons get the boats ready for the next run. The Janes family was deeply involved in the new drug business, and all made a large living participating in it.

He proceeded to get in his son's vehicle, adjusted the seat and mirror, and stopped to clean out the trash left from the night before. Finally, he thought he could get on the road as he put the key in the ignition and turned the key. It paused once. When the truck attempted to start, the truck's cab was engulfed with fire and then was blown into many pieces and hurled up to one hundred feet, resulting in a massive explosion with Mr. Janes inside. All of the home's windows where the truck was parked blew out from the explosion's impact, and the neighbor's houses were rattled. All of Mr. Janes's family, wife, and kids stumbled out of bed, trying to figure out what had happened. Parts of the truck were found on the street and personal belongings that were his sons'. The blast was horrific and rocked the whole neighborhood. And Mr. John Janes was pulled from the truck, and the family soon realized he was severely burned but alive. Help was called immediately. When the ambulance arrived, they realized he needed to be stabilized if there was any chance for him to survive and get him transported to the hospital as quickly as possible. Approximately two hours after the explosion, Mr. John Janes died en route to the hospital.

The news of the explosion awoke most people in the small village on the island. Retaliation was the first reaction, but then reality set in. And they soon realized somebody talked, and all fingers were pointing at Ronnie.

Word spread quickly; more and more people were suspicious when they were told somebody placed a pipe bomb in the truck's exhaust. Others say it was wired to the battery, and Mr. Janes was not the intended target. The truck belonged to Ronnie, but his father was driving it. The local people could not believe the rumors that a local person was a suspect and hurt Mr. Janes. Just as the bomb incident started to set in, they looked across the town and saw a large plume of smoke. Someone yelled that something was burning at the docks. People in the small city scrambled to get over to where the smoke was coming from to see what was on fire. Upon arrival, the townspeople could not believe what they were seeing. Three boats were burning, and it did not look like they could be saved. Latex gloves were dipped in diesel fuel and used as the accelerant when they were set on fire. Once the glove hit the deck, the fuel would spread out to get the fire started. And as anyone knows working around that type of fuel that once it starts burning, there is no putting it out. It burns until there is nothing left. Just as the crowd began to grow where the fire was, Captain Tom looked across the river, and he could see a small boat with no lights on and two men watching from a distance. As he looked closer, he realized he knew one of the men. It was the Columbian man from Miami that had invited him and the crew to the toga party.

Holy shit, Tom thought. *What in the hell is this going to turn into? This is definitely a warning being sent for the local smugglers to keep their mouths shut.*

Now the locals were beginning to turn on each other more and more. Speculation of what had happened and their version were all over the town. Everyone was scared and afraid to speak to anyone.

The bombing was a retaliation move against the smugglers in the business.

The townspeople were unsettled with everyone knowing all the business ends and outs, which they so very much needed to survive. Being related and growing up with each other made this even more challenging, and it was devastating to learn one of their own could have done this to a fellow islander.

Nobody was talking, and the tension in this town was so thick that it split the locals into several groups. They began protecting themselves, and the fighting was soon to follow. It was hard to know who you could trust, and most people were running scared, afraid that they were next if they opened their mouths in any way. Death could happen to any of them in any horrific, painful way. Money is the root of all evil.

When you are looking at a vast amount of jail time and different nationalities clashing in the mix, crazy things can happen.

CHAPTER 14

New Rules of Engagement

The new rule of engagement was now ordering two boats simultaneously, which was essential. These boats would need to be delivered all at the same time but in different locations. One would be dismantled and left to rest on the ocean's sandy bottom, giving it a final resting place, never to come back ashore again. After unloading all of the drugs into smaller boats, that would bring them ashore in different areas. The first boat would be used as a decoy. It would run at a high rate of speed and let the law chase them long enough to allow the other boat to get the drugs inshore. The area they were assigned to brought them into and allowed millions of dollars of cocaine to filter through the main artery that ran through their little fishing village and be distributed all across the United States.

Billy had his hands full with this order running four crews in three different locations and spreading himself through all areas to ensure completion and delivery on time. He vowed this would be his last after the money he would make off this order, and he would retire.

The time was near when Billy moved the boats to the water in Marathon and installed the engines. All decking was in place, and Billy ordered powerful engines to be placed with the specific specification to allow plenty of room to stack the precious cargo for the immense profits to be protected in the run and arrive intact.

"Remember," Billy told his crew. "These are the fastest boats we have ever built. Everything has to be compact to make room for these large engines. We have to make sure everything is perfect. I want to take them out on their first run to break in the engines next week. Get the mechanic here, and let's get her done."

Billy was finishing the daily work done on the boats, making sure they were on schedule. The first evening star started to come out, so Billy knew it was time to call it for the night. On his way home, he stopped by the Elks Lodge and had a couple of drinks when Pete, another man from the Everglades that worked for another crew, walked in looking for Billy and needed to speak to him as soon as possible.

Once outside, Pete began to tell Billy that a drug enforcement agent had boarded his boat, Captain Grizz, and they had not left it yet. Then he proceeded to tell him that a man at the docks that they paid to watch the boat had called him and said to him that he saw the agent put marijuana in the bilge. He witnessed the whole thing. You see, Captain Grizz was a new boat Billy had just completed, and it had made only a handful of legit fishing trips. And this boat had never been used to haul drugs, and they had never had anything on it. In other words, it had only left the dock a few times.

Remember, these guys were men of men, and they sure did not back down from a challenge or fight. Billy was six feet six and solid muscle, and hearing this made him furious. He told Pete to get in the truck. They were going down to the dock. Once they arrived, they saw the agents searching and still checking everything out on the boat.

Billy approached them and yelled, "What the hell are you doing on the boat."

The agent told him he was there to search it.

Billy yelled back, "Do you have a warrant?"

"No, sir, I don't."

Billy then walked down to the dock and got onboard. Billy told the agents, "They had to get off of the boat now."

The agent replied, "We will not."

Just as the agent finished his sentence, Billy hauled off and decked the man. Billy loved a good fight, and he struck the agent with such a significant impact that he flew over the side of the boat and hit the water. The agent, not being familiar with the water, hit some rocks by the dock and cut his arm on the way down. Pete then joined in and hit the other agent standing there. Let's say they both received a complimentary car ride to the local jail where they were both arrested and booked.

After a few hours, and when they were allowed their one phone call, they called Bobby Pete's brother to come and bail them out of jail. Bobby was pissed because he had to get up in the middle of the night and find his pilot to fly him to the Keys and bail Billy and Pete out of jail.

It was now noon, and all the paperwork was processed, and the guys were out. Bobby picked up the jailbirds and drove them to the dock to check on the boat. The judge arraigned them, but the clerks held them just long enough in jail while processing the paperwork to let them out so that the agents could confiscate the boat. Captain Grizz was tagged and already being towed out of the area where it was docked. Captain

Grizz was no more, and it was now the US government's property waiting to be sold at auction. They lost the boat, and it would never be returned to them again unless purchased.

CHAPTER 15

The Business Plan

The drug business was not a normal mom-and-pop business. The business plan associated with this new sophisticated business was very strategic and precise, right to every penny made, and sent back to the sleepy fishing village, making these hardworking men and women some of the newest millionaires of south Florida.

With the new money came new problems. Not knowing how to handle the money was a big issue. People buying new cars and homes paying cash for them did not make this an easy task for the local people. Remember, most were not educated and had never really been out of the area except to fish and return, but most of these men were hardworking and very loyal.

With the new drug trade came a partying level that had never been seen before. Further drug use was an everyday occurrence, and the people were very open about it. Cocaine was the drug of choice, and it was nothing to purchase a half once for the party of the night. But soon, snorting was not enough to keep some of the people riding the high they had become so accustomed to.

Freebasing was the next step to continue the high when snorting could not accommodate. Freebasing is the process base on the salt in which cocaine is naturally found, taking the drug to its purest form. This made the drug extremely potent, and most users run the risk of an overdose if they don't know what they are doing.

There are various methods for free-basing cocaine. The most popular is using a small glass pipe and a small piece of clean heavy copper, which is used as a reduction base so the coke can be melted and boiled until it turns into a vapor. Then the freebase cocaine can be smoked. The users usually feel extreme fatigue, depression, anxiety, and para-noia, to name a few of the common side effects. Long-term use can induce mood changes and hallucinations.

When this addictive drug became such a hot commodity, adding this rec-reational use of the illegal substance to the illicit drug running through the area makes for a dangerous and lethal combination.

CHAPTER 16

Death in the Everglades

Lana, a local girl who worked at a local convenience store, usually worked the evening shift until closing. One evening, Lana was approached and asked if she would be interested in selling a little coke from the store where she worked. After a few minutes, she said she would but did not have the money to start it off.

The two men who had come to her were local men. They were from the Naples area and had a ruthless reputation. She had seen them around throughout the years but never really had any reason to go around them until tonight. The two men were a couple of drug dealers who were referred to as the Clifford brothers that moved many drugs on land and water through the small town.

Lana would pick up an eight ball or two and then cut it, and she would then sell it from the counter in the store for profit. She then paid the Clifford brothers their part and kept the remainder for herself.

Lana would use part of the drugs herself but never too much, so it would not cut into her profits. This also allowed her a little financial freedom to get the things she never had enough money to buy before.

Everything with Lana's small business was going well. It took off and started growing and growing; she needed more and more cocaine to satisfy the supply and demand of her successful business.

Lana always got the drugs fronted to her by the brothers, making this dangerous. The Clifford brothers were not the most honorable people. Some local people would always say that one of the brothers was born in the wrong era because he permanently settled his large or small problems with death and never thought twice about it, and this was who Lana chose to do business with.

One evening, the store was extremely busy. Some men came into the store and had Lana go outside to help him with the gas pump. While outside assisting the customer, one of the men stayed inside the store.

Word traveled fast about what Lana was offering for sale. The man who stayed in the store went behind the counter and stole Lana's stash that was hidden in a special place waiting to be sold; Lana's special hiding place that she always stashed the drugs in and never thought anyone know where it was but her.

The scenario was not a good thing because now she would not have enough money to pay the brothers for the fronted drugs she had in her possession.

Lana only had until the end of the week to cover the debt owed to the brothers. One week passed, and she didn't have it. Lana thought she needed to come clean with them and let them know what had happened. She placed the dreaded call and asked them for a little extra time. They responded that they would go by the store where she worked and talk to her about it later that night.

Nothing was ever discussed on the phone, always in person. Paranoia was normal for anyone dealing with and using this product. The brothers had no intention of going to jail for anyone, which was made very clear from the get-go.

Later that evening, when the brothers arrived, it was late at night and almost closing time. One of the brothers was a businessman, and the other one was very mean looking and quiet, which she was most scared of. She had heard rumors about them killing people who had wronged them, but she was sure she could smooth this over because she didn't steal the drugs; they were stolen from her.

They came into the store well-dressed like professional people. The men smelled so good that it was intoxicating. Both were handsome and well-groomed and enticing that she would love to have for a full night of erotic pleasure with both of them at the same time.

Then he snapped his fingers and got her out of her fog and her attention. The older brother proceeded to ask her for the money she owed them. She then explained to them what had happened.

"I have been robbed. Someone came behind the counter and stole all of the coke. Nothing was left."

"I am going to have to make payments to you until I get it all paid back."

"I will if you just give me a chance and some time."

The brothers asked, "How long do you need? How do we know you didn't party on the drugs yourself?"

"You don't, and you will have to take my word for it." Lana explained, "I have always delivered the money to you and have been honest."

The brothers then asked, how she was getting home.

Lana replied, "I have a friend who is going to give me a ride."

The brothers then told her they will give her a ride. "You don't live far, do you?"

"Sure," Lana responded. "No, I don't live that far."

She called her friend, canceled her ride, closed up the store for the night, and hopped in the truck with them, one brother sitting on each side of her as they drove off.

It was a warm and humid early morning with a little mist in the air when two hunters started walking in the water to a local area looking for deer. Most of the area had water anywhere from two inches to six inches deep and sabal palms sticking up everywhere. After an hour or so, with no luck of a deer, they decided to call it quits but before Alvin decided to check one more area. When they entered this area, there was something hanging from a tree. Alvin and Sammy stumbled across a young woman who had been murdered.

They had no idea who she was because her face was so distorted, not realizing they had found Lana's body chained to a tree where she had been beaten and tortured to death. Some of the things they did to her were so horrific.

Lana had been disemboweled alive, and her insides were lying on the ground. She had hung from the tree bleeding for hours before the men had found her.

The Clifford brothers had no heart, and they sent a strong message to the people of the area that they would not tolerate theft or people running their mouths about them or their business.

Alvin and Sammy were in disbelief; they had never seen anything like this before in their life. They decided to call the park rangers who work closely with the sheriff's office that handles this type of investigation.

Upon arriving at the scene, Officer Sanders immediately corded off the area and deemed this a crime scene.

"This site and the body were so graphic that it would be forever imprinted in my mind for the rest of my life," Officer Sanders said. "We have never encountered anything like this before."

The crime scene investigators had a good idea of who was responsible for this horrific crime. They were notoriously known for the gutting that happened to this poor girl. But like everything else in this town, there was not enough evidence to charge them nor convict them at this time, making this another unsolved murder in the Everglades.

CHAPTER 17

Billy Finalizing
the Boat Order

Today, Billy finalized the order for the two custom yachts bigger than he had ever built with every bell and whistle you could imagine. The secret to this success was to place the boats on each coast once they were completed. Two go-fast boats were on order as well. After three hours of going over all of the specifications, they all agreed. The money was paid, and Billy was to start right away. These boats need to be built as soon as possible. This deal would be one of the biggest hauls in this area to date: one hundred thousand pounds of marijuana and cocaine. Never before has anyone smuggled this amount of drugs all at the same time in one load. This was a game changer. There would be girls on board to sunbathe nude and distract any Coast Guard who might want to board the boat during this haul. They paid top dollar to have these girls run around and entice the men who might be looking. These girls would be expected to do the dirty deed if need-be—strippers by night and not modest at all about their bodies. A crew of four plus the girls make a total of six on the larger boats.

One yacht would be deployed from the West Coast and the other from the Florida Keys with the big boss's destination for the cargo to be dropped; Captain Tom being at the helm of one, and the other was set up as a decoy. Projected build time was a year for the whole order to be complete, and Billy had his hands full getting this done and finding places that people would not expect him to be.

Meanwhile, back in the Florida Keys on a hot beautiful sunny day, one of the new boats was ready for its test run. Captain Tom could not wait to get his hands on the new boat, and when he did, he pushed the new boat to its limits. He needed to see how fast she could go and make sure she could perform to the captain's expectations. This boat was set up with the turbo and the blowers and larger injectors to give it more horsepower. The dynamics of this boat were built for speed. She was made for riding light in the water, and they knew she was just intended to be used for this job, and she could fly.

"Wow," Captain Tom said. "I have never seen anything like this before. Billy, you outdid yourself on this one.

This is the fastest thing I have ever seen on the water."

Billy was on board to make sure all went well, and everything was in working order. This boat was designed to outrun the Coast Guard, or it was designed for the guys to have some fun and play with them a little on the water.

CHAPTER 18

The Largest Haul in the History of Smuggling

In the still of the night, the last of the supplies and instructions had been given to the captains for the largest ride ever to be had in these waters. The sky was clear with no cloud in sight and with the stars looking bright like you can just reach up and grab one. The water was a slick calm just the way Captain Tom liked it.

"A smooth ride for the boys tonight," Tom said.

Tom checked and rechecked his information so that everything was in order before he took off. This time, the boat was leaving the docks out of Marathon instead of the Everglades to keep the attention to a minimum. It was not a full moon, so the luck was on their side, but as they left the dock, you could see the bait and the fish along with the phosphorous lighting up the waterway like someone had turned the lights on to show them the way out. The sky was so bright that they ran with the lights off, trying not to be seen.

The Star Gazer left with the Bluebird, getting ready to hit the high seas within the hour. Both boats met the freighter within thirty minutes of each other just off the western side of Dry Tortuga. One was to load from one side of the freighter, while the other was to load from the opposite side. Tom thought to himself, *Not much traffic out here. It is going to be a smooth ride.*

Just as his thought entered his mind, the spotter plane came on the radio and said, "Captain, it is a beautiful night out tonight. Bring her to the hill."

Tom had thirty thousand pounds of marijuana loaded on the Star Gazer, and as soon as the crew moved it below deck, they took off and headed for Pavilion Key off the Ten Thousand Islands to meet the other boats and offload the cargo as quickly as possible.

The Star Gazer left an hour before the Bluebird. This was to ensure that if they had any problems getting this part of the load, the Bluebird would be home free to bring their cargo to shore safely. The Star Gazer was on approach and did not hear anything when the spotter plane came on and said, "The fishing nets are full, and we are still not seeing any sharks."

Captain Tom came back and said, "Thank you, I am taking her in."

Once at the agreed destination, eight T-Craft came out to meet the Star Gazer to offload five thousand pounds on each of the six boats with the other two keeping watch, making sure no problems would arise. As these boats took off in all different directions, some would go north, some south, and some east. The Bluebird came on the radio thanking the good buddy in the spotter plane and said, "He was heading to the hill."

Now the next six boats were heading out to meet the Bluebird. As the marijuana was offloaded from the Bluebird into the boats, they took off again in all different directions, getting out of sight as quickly as they could just like they had done earlier, except these were going to be off-loaded in Big Pine Key. All of the boats ran at a very high rate of speed except, this time, they were going to travel through the Spanish Channel, which was a narrow pass that was shallow on both sides and deep in the middle. Only local people of the area knew how to navigate through this pass. Everything was going as planned when the last of the T-Craft started into the Spanish Channel, and another T-Craft was coming out of the same area simultaneously. Both boats were traveling at a high rate of speed, and both boats were trying to stay as undetectable as possible when the unthinkable happened: the two boats collided. One was going out empty, and the other was coming in loaded. Neither boat was using their running lights on their boats. This was a common practice to make sure the loads arrived safely.

With the hard impact of the boats colliding, one man was killed instantly, and the other was seriously injured

The watcher boats went into full alert and had to hurry and get up to the Spanish Channel and get a crew to the injured boat and off-load the cargo that had been transported into the area. Now time was of the essence to get it out of there before the marine patrol arrived. Just as the drugs were hidden, the marine patrol who worked with the local sheriff's office arrived on the scene. He investigated and handled the accident from start to finish. The boy's body was nowhere to be found, and it took them three days to recover it from the water where the crash happened.

The crew had all kinds of drugs hidden in the mangroves and stashed all over town. Now the team could breathe a little sigh of relief that this stage of the job was over. Now they waited to move the drugs out to be sold.

News of the tragic loss went across the airways rapidly. Just as Captain Tom learned about the accident, he got word that the decoy yacht had been launched and headed into a different area that was teaming with law enforcement.

Tom thought to himself, *What a tragic loss of good people. I hope that the decoy boat knows what they are doing.*

Now the decoy boat named Barbara Ann was playing with some crab traps on the boat's deck. They wrapped two of them together in a burlap sack and made it look like a bale of marijuana. They stacked twenty fake bales on the deck, and they continued to party with the girls on deck to see who might be looking at them. They made a couple of passes close to a couple of local fishermen who was working that night to see if they could catch their attention. After a few passes, they went about their business, and one of the ladies they had hired to call the Coast Guard reported seeing a boat with bales of pot on it running through an area known for smuggling.

Within forty-five minutes, a Coast Guard boat was chasing them through the waterways. The captain was very experienced and was hauling ass through the area like it was his playground. After chasing the Barbara Ann for twenty minutes through the passes, the Coast Guard could not gain any ground, so he called for backup. Within an additional twenty minutes, a helicopter was hovering above the boat, demanding them to stop.

Just as a Coast Guard boat came up to the side of the bow, the captain of the Barbara Ann could see he had pissed the Coast Guard off to the max. He noticed guns had been drawn, and the captain came on the loudspeaker and demanded the boat to stop.

Little did the Coast Guard know that during their chase of the decoy, the Vikki Ann had already picked up their cargo and headed to rendezvous with the two go-fast boats and took the load into the Florida Keys.

The Vikki Anne was gorgeous—a yacht dressed with everything imaginable to make this one of the most luxurious trips. The yacht was even outfitted with some of the most valuable cargo a boat could carry. This job was worth millions of dollars, and they took no chances to make sure the drugs were unloaded in a timely fashion into two go-fast boats to bring it ashore as quickly as they could.

Twenty thousand pounds of marijuana with five thousand pounds cocaine in the center wrapped around it with their favorite bud was loaded into each boat. Both captains, very experienced with the water around Marathon Key, made this a breeze. One at a time, the boats made the drop-off at the local rock pit where two front-end loaders were waiting to place the drugs in dump trucks and haul it out to their final destination in Miami.

The first boat named Party Time was early, and the guys were waiting for them. The front-end loaders went down in the water, and the crew formed a human cargo line and started stacking the bales in the bucket until it was full. The first front-end loader retreated and went up the hill to where a dump truck was waiting, and he dumped the drugs into the back-end of the truck. The other was soon to follow as quickly as possible until they had enough to fill it halfway. They took gravel and covered it up to make sure it wasn't visible, and then one of the front-end loaders went back and pushed the boat out into the deeper water so it could take off and get out of there.

The Linda T was soon to arrive with the same cargo on board. The crew quickly repeated the same routine to get the drugs out of the area and on the road safely to the destination in Miami.

With the cargo heading out to the final location for distribution, Benny, the boat captain of the Vikki Ann, had one more thing to complete before heading home. It was time to take the Vikki Ann on her final voyage and to her final resting spot far below the beautiful, clear water down to depths unknown to lay on the sandy bottom of the ocean floor, never to be seen again. She did her job and did it very well.

CHAPTER 19

The Boat Chase

At a high rate of speed, the Coast Guard was in full pursuit of the Star Gazer with Captain Tom at the helm. They came over the radio and ordered them to slow and then to stop. Captain Tom refused to slow; he hit it with full throttle. As Captain Tom was in the process of out-running them, shots rang out, and the cutter drew down on the boat and told them to stop, or they will open fire. Just as Captain Tom thought he was clear to run, another cutter ran right in front of the bow, and shots rang out again across the bow. That was when Tom came to a complete stop. He looked up and realized he had a gunboat in front, aiming at them with another at the stern.

Over the radio, they came on and said they were going to board the boat and search it. They asked all of the crew and the captain to lay face down on the deck with their hands where they could be seen. The crew and Tom did as they were instructed.

The Coast Guard had no love for Captain Tom and his crew. The sergeant had been trying to catch Tom for years and took this very personally. The sergeant had felt like Tom and his crew made him look incompetent to his superiors.

The Coast Guard made Tom and his crew lie face down on their bellies for hours in the hot, sweltering sun to make it as uncomfortable as possible.

The men were beginning to get sunburned as they lay there in the heat of the day. They asked if they could use the restroom, and they were told no until one of the crew members soiled himself. Finally, they allowed him to stand and be humiliated in front of everyone.

Just as they allowed them to stand, they were handcuffed to the side of the boat and told not to move. The crew did as they were told, fearing retaliation for what they were doing out there. They were told, "Please be brave and try something because I would love to shoot you and get it over with and save the taxpayers a lot of money."

Finally, Tom and the crew were arrested and taken to jail.

The harassment was at its highest. The boat had been cleaned from end to end. The crew had made sure nothing was on it because of what had happened before. As long as the captain and the crew keep their head on straight and their mouths shut and say nothing, they would have to be released because there was no evidence.

Tom knew Frank Anderson, their attorney, would come in and represent them. With no visible evidence, he demanded that the captain and the crew be released at once.

After six hours of being locked up, they finally agreed they had to let them go.

Captain Tom told the crew, "Let's go home and get some rest. We can talk about it tomorrow."

CHAPTER 20

~~~~~~

The Bluebird
Takes the Lead

Another job was soon to be on the horizon. This time, the Star Gazer would be left behind at the docks. The Bluebird was taken out of the dry dock and placed in the water.

The crew did their standard chores and was heading to the port to get fuel and supplies. Kent had a meeting with the crew to make sure everyone was on the same page. The last thing he needed was someone wigging out on the boat. Kent told the crew the trip was estimated to be a week long. Anyone who did not want to make the trip could leave now with no questions asked. Kent would understand, given the heat and harassment that had come down on them the past couple of times being out on the water. All the crew agreed to do the job and take the money offered.

Kent said, "Let's get her loaded. We want to be out of here by 3:00 a.m. Make sure the Bluebird has everything we need, and she is fired up and ready to go by the time I get here. I'm going home to get some sleep. I'll see you guys in the morning."

The Bluebird was dressed with a standard mackerel gill net, looking as though she was ready to go fishing. They placed fish crates under the net to make them look like it was running with a full net onboard. Still, they only had two hundred yards of the net onboard. Little did the Coast Guard know the fish they were fishing for is called a square grouper, which was thirty thousand pounds of redbud marijuana coming in from Columbia.

Kent arrived at the dock and started doing his once-over of the engine and boat, making sure she was in tip-top shape because he knew he would be pushing her to her limits on this trip. The marine patrol and the Coast Guard were everywhere, and Kent and the crew knew they could not play around out there, and they had to return to shore as fast as they could.

It was a beautiful and clear, full moonlit night. The air was cool, blowing a northwest breeze, making it a little chilly to be on the water. Kent arrived at the dock and was dry heaving, which was a normal routine until he got on the boat and started out of the canal that led to the Gulf of Mexico. With no boats in sight, Kent began with his prayers as he began to run the boat slow and easy with no lights until they got offshore.

Kent prayed for the crew to come home safe, and he prayed for the safety of the trip, and then he concluded with all of the men being returned to their families and not going to jail. Kent sped the boat up, and he felt like he was the king of the road, with them being the only boat in sight. They had a full day to get to the freighter they were meeting just south of the Marquesas.

Right on schedule, Captain Kent said as he looked out the front windshield with the binoculars.

Kent yelled at the crew, "Get ready." The mother ship was here with the load.

Captain Kent went on the radio and said, "Lion, Lion, Lion, I am here, come back. Lion, Lion, Lion, I see you. Left side, please, sir."

Kent proceeded to the left side of the freighter. Still moving at a slow rate of speed, positioning the Bluebird perfectly as he pulled up along the side of her. A crane lowered the first five thousand pounds wrapped in a cargo net and placed it on the deck, and then the second was soon to follow with the third and fourth following that. Captain Kent came on the radio and said, "Thank you, and I'll see you on the flip side."

Kent hit the throttles, raised the Bluebird's hydrofoils that she was so notorious for, and took off. He told the crew he would like it left on the deck because he had several boats coming out to meet them. Just as Kent was taking off, they spotted a plane in the sky. Kent knew this plane did not belong to the group of people he worked with. After watching for several minutes, he heard the plane start to spit and sputter. Then they saw some smoke starting to come from one of the engines, and the plane began to lose altitude. Just as they looked out the window, they could see the plane was attempting to land on its belly on the water. The plane bounced back and forth and finally came to a complete stop without tearing the plane's body apart. The pilot was alive, and they could see he was attempting to open the door. The impact was hard, and you could tell he was beaten up, bruised, and struggling with getting out of the plane.

Finally, he opened the door and was standing on the wing, holding his head. Kent had no choice but to turn and head toward the plane and see if he needed help.

Upon arrival, Kent could see the pilot waving his arms at him and blood dripping down his face. Kent opened the window and yelled at the pilot, "Are you okay?"

"Yes, I'm okay, beat up but good."

Kent asked, "Do you have anyone coming to help you?"

The pilot responded, "No, and I need your help."

Kent replied, "Well, let's get you on board and patched up."

When the pilot came on board, Kent introduced himself and learned his name was David, and he lived in Marathon and carried 12,000 pounds of hash from Columbia. He asked if he could help him with it, and he would split the profits. Kent agreed and told the crew to get on that plane and move the drugs as quickly as possible. Kent then explained to David that the law enforcement agencies were horrible right now, and they needed to get a move on before someone sees them. After all of the drugs, David came on board the Bluebird, and Captain Kent raised the hydrofoils and started the trip home.

The Bluebird made it twenty miles offshore of Key West, and the Coast Guard was in full pursuit. Kent knew he could maneuver through the shallow waterways in and around the area. He just needed a few more minutes to reach them. The Bluebird was making her way to East Bahia Honda to a channel mainly known and used by the locals, so they could easily pass through and get where they needed to be. The Coast Guard would not take a chance of going through this passage with their bigger vessels. There would be a big chance the vessel would not make it through such shallow waters and run aground. Kent called the smaller boats that he was meeting and said that he was about twenty minutes away from them. And he didn't know if he was going to make it to the destination because he had sharks behind him, and he didn't want to drag them to the boat.

"We have a big problem, the sharks are everywhere and are eating us alive."

Captain Tom heard the radio call, and he came on and said, "I am en route."

Kent asked that they get here as quickly as possible. After fifteen minutes, Captain Tom showed up in a go-fast boat to help save the load. Tom ran the long skinny boat right up to the side of the Bluebird while it was still running at a high rate of speed, and they linked up. And Tom told the crew to start throwing some bales for him to stack on the go-fast boat to get it out of there as quickly as possible. Captain Kent yelled at Tom and tried to fill him in on what had happened.

"We have an extra person and twelve hundred pounds of hash to add to the drop."

Captain Tom responded, "Do you have any more fucking surprises for me?"

"No, that's it for now," Kent responded.

After half of the bales and the hash were thrown to the go-fast boat. All other boats took off in different directions. Some had drugs on them, and some did not. The boats without the drugs were used as a decoy to get the Coast Guard to chase them so they could bring the Bluebird to the docks safely.

With ten thousand pounds of marijuana left on the bluebird's deck, Kent approached the seven-mile bridge with all running lights on, brought her into Marathon seafood well after dark, and backed her into a boat slip often used for local lobster fishermen.

Several rows of traps were stacked on land where the Bluebird was docked, so the crew unloaded and stacked the bales in the middle of the traps, making the drugs remarkably camouflaged until they could be moved out of the area to be sold.

As soon as Kent moved the Bluebird away from Marathon seafood, the vans moved in to collect the bales and the hash out of the traps and sent them on the road to their final destination as quickly as possible for a very good night's work.

CHAPTER 21

Floating in the Ocean

What a gorgeous day. The water was slick calm, and it looked just like glass. The visibility was so clear that you could see straight to the bottom.

What a day to be out on the beautiful Atlantic Ocean side of Marathon on my favorite beach I enjoy when I'm not working, Tom thought.

What started out as a relaxing day turned when his phone rang, and he could see it was Mario Gonzalez. Tom had to answer, and at the end of the call, he wished he hadn't. Mario told Tom to go to the airport. He was there on a plane waiting to speak to him and to pack a light bag; he would be gone for a couple of days.

Most fishermen are superstitious, and this day was a little different than the others. Tom had a knot in his stomach, which almost made him feel sick. He was feeling a bit uneasy about his unexpected trip like something terrible was going to go wrong. Leaving from the Atlantic side was not unusual, but departing from the Bahamas was. Tom tried to cancel the job for a week or so until this passed, but with no luck, the big boss put an extreme amount of pressure on him to keep this job on schedule. He explained to Tom that the other boat captain they used was coming in with the load and had a massive heart attack, and the job was vulnerable because of the attention it caused. Mario would not take no for an answer and demanded the pilot to take them to Andros Island off the Bahamas to get Tom on board the boat that he would be commanding later that day.

When they arrived, he could see the boat was a go-fast boat, and it had two crew members, and with him made three. The boat was sitting at the dock tied up, and she was loaded and ready to go. Tom knew a boat like this could run at top speed. He asked the crew to help him check the engine and make sure they are in tip-top shape and ready to run. Tom did his once-over and agreed to the job and told the boys, "Let's get our stuff on board and push off. We are burning daylight out here."

Mario was shocked at how professional Tom handled the job, and soon he was taken back to the airport for his return flight home. As the plane took off, Tom looked up in the sky and wished he was on it and not on this boat.

On this trip, it was a straight shot to Fort Pierce for unloading. Tom thought it should take them ten hours tops from start to finish. As the boat started pulling away from the island and into the open waters, it was a little choppy, but the boat was running well at first. Then Tom noticed a slight drag on the engine. As he went further offshore, he noticed the engine starting to bog down. Tom immediately checked the boat's bilge and found that it was taking on water.

Tom then told the crew, "The boat was taking on more water than I want. We needed to get the pumps started and get her pumped out."

Tom then noticed the water was more than what he had originally thought. The boat became sluggish and seemed as though it was struggling when one of the crew finally spoke up and told Tom that the Bahamian Coast Guard had chased them right up on a shelf with very little water, and the boat had bottomed out a couple of times.

Tom was pissed and said, "It would have been nice for you to tell me that back at the dock."

Tom now realized the boat's hull was starting to split open, and they needed to get to shore as quickly as possible. They were too far to turn back, so they had no choice but to keep going and pray they make it.

They were now twenty miles off the coast of Florida heading toward Fort Pierce when the unthinkable happened. The hull of the boat cracked completely open, and it only took about ten minutes, and she sank completely out of sight. The crew had no time to get floating devices for themselves to get in or even put life preservers on. Everything on the boat was gone.

Tom thought three grown men were now treading water fifteen or twenty miles off the coast from where they needed to bring the load ashore safe and sound. Hopefully, they would start looking for them after a couple of hours passed when they were supposed to arrive.

CHAPTER 22

Survival Mode

Now three men were floating in the water at depth of one thousand feet to six thousand feet of water, trying to hang on for dear life.

Tom gathered all three together and said, "Everyone needs to stay close." Tom then ordered the crew, "Empty your pockets, especially anything with a smell. Then you guys need to take off any shiny jewelry that sparkles in the water."

Tom said, "You guys need to listen to me, we are in survival mode, and you need to pay attention. Anything that shines looks like food to these bigger fish that swim out here. We don't want to attract any attention to anything passing by."

Tom took his gold chain off and his watch and held them in his hand for a few minutes, remembering who had bought them for him and how much he loved her. He then let go of them and watched them sink out of sight. Tom was still daydreaming when he heard a big swish, and the water popped like something had hit it with force. Then by the grace of God, he looked over his shoulder to see six of the bales of pot that they were hauling popping up on the surface of the water.

Tom said to himself, *Thank you, Lord. I knew they were airtight.* "This will give us something to float on until we are rescued. We are not that far off-shore. Someone will send help."

As the day started to turn to night, Tom and the crew knew this was feeding time, and they had to be diligent about keeping an eye out for predators. Tom told the crew they needed to take turns sleeping, and one will have to keep watch.

As the night sky fell into a deep purple color with pink and blue streaks in it from the sun setting, the men could see each other's faces clearly in the moonlight. The moon was shining bright, and it looked a little cloudy and overcast, and they had no idea what time it was. All they knew was they were exhausted and had been floating since early that afternoon and were scared of becoming a meal for a large fish or prey passing by.

Tom played the scenario of everything that had happened repeatedly in his head as he floated on the bale of marijuana. All of the warning signs were there about not going on this job, and the feeling he had was deep and hard. Tom felt guilty because he knew he should not have taken this job. If something happens to any of these men, it might be a little more than he could handle. Tom felt it was his fault, and it could cost him or the crew.

Just as he was deep in that thought, he felt a bump in the middle of his back. Tom spun around and saw nothing. Clouds covered the moon. It was too dark on the water's surface to identify what was doing it, and that was when a second bump came with more force than the first. Tom told the crew to be on the lookout. Tom stuck his head underwater, attempting to identify the fish, and saw a seven-foot blacktip shark swimming right at him. They test their prey with their nose by bumping it to see if they want to eat it. Just as the third pass was about to happen, Tom took his pocketknife out of his pocket and stabbed the shark in the eye. The shark retreated, leaving a lot of blood that had filled the area they were floating in.

Tom told the guys, "I know you are tired, but we have to get out of this blood trail and need out of it now. So kick your feet as hard as you can, and let's move our makeshift raft."

The guys continued to kick for about an hour. When they thought they were clear, only then did they rest.

Tom said, "That was a close one. Is everyone okay?"

Both men answered and said, "We are good, Captain."

One man said, "I have a scrape on my arm as the shark passed, it rubbed up against me pretty hard. That skin is rough like stiff sandpaper."

Tom replied, "It will cut you like a knife. Keep your arm up and out of the water as much as you can, and make sure it stops bleeding. We don't need anything following us."

"It's too late, Captain. There is a big fin right behind you, breaking the water."

Tom spun around to look and could see it was a massive hammerhead shark. That shark seemed to be a good fifteen feet long, and it could turn from side to side very quickly. Every time they think it was going away from them, it turned and came back at them again.

"This is not going to be fun."

Finally, one of the men got close enough to the snout and punched it as hard as he could when its head breached the water.

He said, "I don't know if this is going to help us or hurt us."

The shark retreated with fury. Tom took a deep breath and told the guys, "Well, we got lucky with that one if he stays gone."

As day broke and the sun came out, the three men floating in the ocean were very hungry and weak. Captain Tom had some survival training, and it was time to put it into action. He told the guys to grab the seaweed he saw floating by. The two boys looked at him like he was crazy.

Tom told them, "Grab it, and I will show you. Whatever you do, do not drink the seawater. I don't care how thirsty you are. You can't do that. It will make you dehydrate faster and make you crazy."

When they pulled the seagrass closer, Tom grabbed it and shook it out on top of his makeshift floatation device, which happened to be a bail of marijuana. When he did, out came a bunch of tiny shrimp and crab. Tom looked at the crew and said, "This isn't the Ritz, but it will have to do. Enjoy your breakfast."

Tom would not eat until he made sure the guys had theirs first. A captain is responsible for their crew, and he always had to make sure their safety comes before his own.

The crew told Tom, "Come on, Captain, there is plenty here. We all need to eat."

Tom looked up at the sky and told the guys, "Hey, it looks like a rain shower is not far off. This will be our chance to get a fresh drink of water. Hold on and stay close in case the storm is stronger than what I can see."

Tom was right; it started as a quiet and mild storm but then progressed into a storm with larger waves and choppy seas and a little lightning and thunder to follow. The guys held on to each other's bales as they opened their mouths and drank the water coming down on top of them. It felt so good to cool the skin exposed to the elements, and the best part of all was getting to rinse the salt from the sea off their faces and rehydrate their bodies by devouring the rainwater. Tom thought this was God's way of protecting them, and he said his prayers and thanked him for allowing them to survive so far. And now he prayed for him to help them get ashore safe and to let everyone return to their families.

Chapter 23

The Rescue

After three days of floating in the water, the people who Tom worked for and who he was supposed to turn the drugs over to finally notified the big boss that they had a big problem. The boat was now almost four days overdue. The boat and crew were missing. No signs of boat, wreckage, or the crew were visible for miles. The man in charge told Mario that they have sent boats out to look for them in the area, and they thought they should have been in but had no luck. Mario told them they had no choice but to contact the Coast Guard.

The US Coast Guard was soon contacted, and they put an all-points bulletin out on the boat and the missing men looking for wreckage or survivors.

Within hours, Tom and the crew could hear the helicopter off in the distance from where they were floating. As time passed, they could hear it getting closer and closer. Tom took this time to talk to the crew. He explained they could let the bales go before rescuing and allowing them to float away from them so no contraband would be in their possession. Still, with his knowledge of the equipment the Coast Guard has, he could bet they already had pictures of them floating on their makeshift illegal raft. Then if that was not bad enough, the big fear was they would let the bales go. And Tom thought to himself, *Would I dare take a chance of the helicopter not seeing us in the water and passing us over?* Then Tom and the crew stood a big chance they could drown from fatigue. Until finally, it hovered right above them. Tom thought, *Thank you, Lord, for protecting me and my crew.* Tom and the crew only then breathed a big sigh of relief. The crew was forever grateful when they saw the big whirlybird right on top of them and staying with them the whole time.

The Coast Guard team sent the basket down one at a time and extracted each of the men out of the water. Once in the air, they could see small stuff from the boat still floating in this big, massive sea that had swallowed them up like they were nothing.

Forever grateful for the rescue, when Tom looked out the window, he saw a Coast Guard cutter retrieving the bales of marijuana that were floating on from where they were rescued. Tom knew now he had no chance of staying out of jail.

The chase was over, and it was game over for him. Tom was glad they were out of the water, shriveled, dehydrated, and exhausted but delighted to be alive.

As the helicopter approached the landing pad, they could see all DEA agents and local law enforcement officers lined up to arrest them. Cop cars were visible with all the flashing lights waiting for them.

CHAPTER 24

The Arrest

Once the helicopter landed, each man was led to the side door where they were met by DEA agents one at a time and handcuffed and placed in separate vehicles where they would be transported to jail and be processed.

After being stripped, searched, and placed in a holding cell, Tom started looking around and started to take it all in. That was when reality began to settle in. Finally, Tom took a deep breath and realized how relieved he was not having to look over his shoulder all the time or worrying about being arrested, and he knew this would get him out of the dreaded contraband hauling. With all the money he made and the fancy lifestyle he and his family lived, this was the reality for his life for the next twenty years. Dark, dingy, cold, and ugly was the best way to describe the cell they were being held in until the arraignment.

Tom also knew if there was any chance of him surviving this arrest, he needed to contact his attorney, Frank, as quickly as he could. Tom was anxious to speak with Frank, and this was where they could sit and discuss the charges. He could also let him know what they had on him and how bad it truly was.

Tom finally contacted Frank, and he agreed to meet with him. He came up to the jail to visit with Tom and go over the charges before the arraignment. Once he was there, he told Tom how serious the charges were and how far they went back.

He told Tom he was looking at some serious time—easy twenty to twenty-five years minimum. Tom told Frank he spoke to the other crew members for them to blame him and put the heat on his back for the job. That way, it would give them minimum sentences. The crew was told they would get taken care of with the attorney's fees and bail as long as they kept their mouths shut about anything else.

Tom asked, "What do you think they will have to serve?"

The attorney replied, "I think they will be sentenced to three years each and probably be out in eighteen months or less."

Tom shook his head in agreement and said, "It is what it is, and we all knew it was coming."

Frank told Tom to sit tight since he had them in line to go in front of the judge to set bail. Tom and the crew were called in for their turn. Since it was their first offense, the judge told the crew he would put the bail at fifty thousand dollars each. The prosecutor had no problem with that and agreed. Then it was Tom's turn. The prosecutor jumped up and asked for him to be remanded with no bail. The prosecutor explained that Tom had plenty of money and means to disappear without a trace. The judge then looked at Tom and said this was his first offense as well.

"Mr. Charles, you can surrender your passport, and you will have a probation officer assigned to you and will have to check in once a week. And you will have to let them know every time you go fishing and where. The bail will be set at five hundred thousand dollars." The judge hit the mallet and said, "Next case."

Tom had Frank arrange all of the bond specifications, and he and the crew were processed out of jail and headed home.

CHAPTER 25

Freedom

Tom arrived home quiet and humble, then he looked around. He saw all of the hard work and the pressure put on him to do the jobs and do them well and provide for the family in a way they could only imagine. Now he stood a chance of losing it all. His family could be worse off than when they started if he didn't handle this right. Tom pulled all of his assets together and was going through each one of them. Most of the property's significant pieces were purchased in his son's name and placed in a trust for him. Now all he had to do was secure the cash he had set aside for him.

The following morning, Tom went to the bank where he had an old family friend and a safe deposit box where he placed the cash.

Tom told Sam, "You have known me for a very long time and know how I like to have things handled off the books. Please, this box is for my son. If something should happen to me, it will be given to him when he turns eighteen years old. Not a day sooner."

Inside the box, Tom wrote his son a letter explaining why he did what he did and how important it was for him not to squander the money in the box and that he had a financial adviser that would help him and teach him how it needed to be handled. In closing, he told him how much he loved him and how he was everything to him and to please forgive him for what he had done. Maybe someday they would see each other again.

That very evening, just as it started to turn to evening, Tom went down to the docks and told the crew's first mate to ready the Star Gazer with food and fuel. He threw a couple of large duffel bags on the boat and asked him to place them in the wheelhouse. After he did that, he wanted him to move the boat down to Big Pine Key where he would tie her up at a certain dock they used.

Tom went back to the house, sat on the couch, and watched Sara in the kitchen as she prepared dinner. Sara was a beautiful woman with a great body, and she did everything he pretty much asked. While watching her, all he could think of was how he wanted to make mad passionate love to the love of his life that was mad as hell for him for the trouble he got all of them in.

Finally, Tom got the nerve up and walked into the kitchen where Sara was cooking. He spun her around and had her look into his eyes. She pulled back, and he grabbed her again and said softly, "Sara, stop. I need to explain why I did what I did and need you now more than ever to understand."

Sara melted into his arms and started to weep. Tom bent down and kissed her passionately on her lips, moved over to her cheeks, and worked down to her neck. That was the one department Tom and Sara had no issues with. As Tom reached her cleavage, he said, "I think your dress is in the way." He untied the wraparound dress she always liked to wear around him for easy access. Like always, no panties or bra were visible. Tom moaned and said, "Just the way I like it." He put Sara on the kitchen counter and made every effort to please her in any way that she had wanted. Sara was hot and wet and moaned with pure passionate pleasure. Tom could always tell when she was ready for the full encounter.

Tom made love to her like it was the last time he would ever see her again. When they finished, he grabbed her and held her for a long time, not saying a word. They both knew what each other was thinking but never made a sound.

Sara loved Tom with her whole heart, and she knew what Tom did for a living and knew this day would come, but she was not completely prepared for it to happen. They never discussed anything. It was the unspoken. A subject danced around for years, but she never wanted to put pressure on him to fill her in, and she did not want to know for her safety. The people in Miami that Tom worked for have been in the news with a lot of speculation about what they do or what they have done. She made sure to keep her distance from that, and she did not want to be in the middle of any of it.

As the afternoon turned to evening, and the sun was setting, the sky was so romantic and beautiful. Sara and Tom sat out on the porch drinking wine, enjoying each other's company, and watched the sunset blasting the sky with some of the most beautiful colors that could be seen. Only in the Florida Keys do they have skies that put out those color combinations as the sun went down, and they were spectacular.

Now the evening turned to night, and Tom and Sara finally started to talk. Tom explained how much he loved her and what she meant to him and how great their life had been, and he could not have asked for anything better. Sara started to cry and asked what would happen to him because this felt like him telling her goodbye, and she was not sure she could handle that right now.

Tom then told her he had left some stuff on the boat and needed to get it.

Sara asked, "Are you going to be a while?"

Tom replied, "No, it should not take me more than an hour."

"Well, hurry home. I have a few more things to show you tonight."

Tom looked at Sara with a long gaze and said, "I will, I promise."

Tom got in his truck, started it, and backed out of the driveway. As he got onto the road, he stopped and looked at the house and its surroundings. Tom then put his truck into gear and drove off slowly with a tear rolling down his cheek. Sara stood close to the window and watched as he drove slowly away.

Tom drove to Big Pine, and as he arrived at the dock, there was the Star Gazer. She was fired up and warm, just waiting for him to come aboard and take command. Tom thought to himself, *She has never failed me, and tonight we are going to test her to her limit.* The first mate, John, met Tom at the truck and asked if there was anything else he needed loaded and if he wanted him to go fishing with him.

Tom replied, "No, not on this trip. I'm going alone." Tom then asked, "Do you have the extra fuel onboard?"

"Yes," John replied. "Just like you asked."

"Great," Tom said, "then we are good to go."

John knew right then that this would be the last time he ever saw Tom again. John thanked Tom, and then Tom asked him to move his truck and take it back to his house to get it away from the dock.

John agreed and said that he would get it taken care of. "Well, Captain, we had a good ride. You are one of the best, and I want to thank you for everything you have done for my family and me." John hugged Tom and said, "I love you, Brother. Be safe out there. If you ever come back this way, look me up. I would love to work with you again."

Tom got on the boat, and John watched as he took command of her from the wheelhouse. John cast off the ropes as Tom put her in gear and eased her away from the docks, heading to the open seas. John stayed and watched until the boat was out of sight, and he could no longer hear the engine noise as it rode off into the darkness, never to be seen again. No lights were shinning, and no wake or foam was coming from behind the boat, leaving no trail.

A month in time had passed. No sign of Tom or the Star Gazer had been seen or reported. Sara had gone on the best she could. When she got in her car to go to work the next day after Tom had not come home, she found a huge duffel bag in her front seat. Sara thought, *What in the world is that?* When she opened it, the bag was full of money. More money than she had ever seen in her life. A note was on the top of the bag, and it said:

> Sara, I love you more than you know. I am so sorry for putting you through this. This will take care of you for the rest of your life. Be careful with the way you spend it.
>
> Love, Tom

Now days went by, and rumors had been going through town with all sorts of speculation on what happened to Tom. One was Tom committed suicide, and he was no longer with them.

Some said the cartel from Miami had him killed and cut his body up and fed it to the fish. Some said he went to Columbia, a country he knew very well, and met many people there and were still friends with.

Still, others say he had been seen in Costa Rica and Belize lying on the beach in a bungalow drinking one of the frozen tropical drinks the country is so known for, all the while with a beautiful younger woman lying beside him, soaking up the sun and working on his tan.

REFERENCES

Websites

ABC News. www.abcnews.go.com

Amazon. www.amazon.com.

Archiveofourown. www.archieveofourown. org.

Bleeping Computer. www.bleeping-computer.com.

BrainyQuote www.brainyquote.com.

Coldfear. www.coldfear.com.

Daily Kos. www.dailykos.com.

Dictionary.com. www.acronyms.the-freeddictionary.com.

Facebook. www.facebook.com.

FanFiction. www.fanfiction.com.

Florida News Network. www.fnnon-linefloridanewnetwork.com.

Google. www.sites.google.com.

Justia. www.justia.com.

Miami Herald. www.miamiherald.com.

Naples Daily News. www.naplesdaily-news.com.

POLITICO. www.politico.com.

RawStory. www.rawstory.com.

Reading Quest. www.readingquest.com.

Reddit. www.reddit.com.

Rough Park Press. www.roughpark-press.com.

Sant Barbara News-Press. www.news-press.com.

Subzin. www.subzin.com.

ThreadCurve. www.threadcurve.com.

Tri-cities Business News. www.tricities-businessnews.com.

United Press International. www.UPI.com.

Wattpad. www.wattpad.com.

Wikipedia. www.wikipedia.org.

WordPress. www.worldpress.com.

ABOUT THE AUTHOR

 Barbara Tyner Hall is a mother of three wonderful and grown children and a true entrepreneur at heart who is eager to show her passion for writing about all sorts of stories that she has encountered through her travels, hard work, and imagination. She has a unique talent and style that can place you in the story through her compelling and descriptive writing without leaving your home. Barbara divides her time between her two favorite states, Texas and Florida, where she writes full-time.

Printed in the USA
CPSIA information can be obtained
at www.ICGtesting.com
LVHW051933091123
763520LV00048B/609

9 781662 477737